GUNNING THE ENGINES

"Did you see anyone following us?" Frank asked, joining Joe in the parking garage.

"No," Joe replied. "What's up?"

Before Frank could answer, the stillness was shattered by a thunderous rumble. A half second later a black TransAm burst from the access ramp. Like some great hungry beast seeking its prey, it zeroed in on the Hardys.

Frank and Joe dove in opposite directions, the TransAm missing them by inches.

Two men jumped from the car. They were the same height and wore identical gray suits. Dark sunglasses hid their eyes. They were mirror images of each other, except for their hair—and the guns they aimed at Frank and Joe.

Books in THE HARDY BOYS CASEFILES® Series

Available from ARCHWAY Paperbacks

THE HARDY BOYS CASEFILES NO. 36

RUNNING ON EMPTY

FRANKLIN W. DIXON

AN ARCHWAY PAPERBACK
Published by POCKET BOOKS

New York   London   Toronto   Sydney   Tokyo   Singapore

AN ARCHWAY PAPERBACK *Original*

An Archway Paperback published by
POCKET BOOKS, a division of Simon & Schuster Inc.
1230 Avenue of the Americas, New York, NY 10020

ISBN: 0-671-74107-1

First Archway Paperback printing February 1990

10 9 8 7 6 5 4 3

RUNNING ON EMPTY

Chapter

1

"BLAST HIM, FRANK!" Joe Hardy yelled, his blue eyes flashing.

With deadly aim, Frank Hardy squeezed the trigger and let loose a stream of lethal bullets. A look of surprise and horror grew on the face of the man on the receiving end of Frank's gun burst.

"Yeah!" Joe shouted as the man leapt into the air and crashed to the ground—dead. "That should set the record."

Frank stepped back from the video machine and smiled. A computerized metallic voice chirped, "You have achieved a ninety-eight percent accuracy rate, ThugBuster. Please put your initials into the ThugBuster Hall of Fame."

"Ho-hum." Frank faked a yawn as he

brushed back his brown hair. He pressed the trigger on the game's joystick and punched in FH1—Frank Hardy, Number One. He turned with a mock bow and offered the machine to his younger brother.

"That won't last long," Joe declared as he stepped up to the machine. He pressed the play button and immediately began blasting away at the cartoon thugs in a high-speed car chase through a cartoon city.

"You two waste more time *and* money trying to outdo each other on these stupid games," said a bored Callie Shaw. She turned away from the machine.

"Why the faraway look?" asked Frank as he slipped an arm around Callie's waist. Actually he knew why. Callie was leaving on a two-week cruise with her parents the following morning, and she didn't want to waste a Friday evening watching Frank and Joe play video games at the Bayport Mall's video arcade center.

"What do you think is taking Chet so long?" Callie asked, ignoring Frank's question.

Frank took his arm from around Callie and cleared his throat. "I don't know. Joe said he was excited about something. You know Chet. He probably found a great new restaurant."

They all knew Chet Morton well. He loved food and disdained any form of physical labor.

As tall as Frank but much heavier, Chet was to the Hardys what a good solid lineman was to a running back—big and slow but always there when needed most. He had stepped in on more than one occasion to help Frank and Joe out of a dangerous situation.

What Chet Morton lacked in speed and motivation, he more than made up for in loyalty and heart.

"What do you think his big surprise is?" Callie asked.

"No telling," Frank replied. "Joe talked to him on the phone. All Chet said was that he wanted us to meet him out front at six o'clock."

"It's six now," Callie declared without looking at her watch.

Whatever Chet's surprise was, Frank thought, it would be a welcome break from crime fighting. Their father, Fenton Hardy, the world-famous private detective, and mother were vacationing, and things were nice and quiet around the Hardy home for a change.

"Hey! You two interested in my score or what?" Joe cut in.

"There he is," Callie announced, ignoring Joe.

Frank followed Callie's finger and was surprised to see Chet squeezing out of a classic maroon Corvette.

Before Frank could say anything, Callie was bounding out the front door.

"Come on, Joe. Chet's here. And wait until you see his new toy," Frank said.

"Hey, can't you wait?" Joe called out as he ran after Frank and Callie. "I almost beat—"

"Hey, guys! What's happening?"

Chet leaned against the maroon Corvette, arms folded, one leg crossed over the other, a sly grin on his face. His clothes looked new and pressed—a drastic change for Chet, who usually wore whatever was on top of the pile on his bedroom floor.

"What lottery did you win?" Frank asked as he walked around the Vette.

"Win?" Chet replied. "My friends. Haven't I always said that hard work is its own reward?"

"Hard work? You?" Callie asked with raised eyebrows.

Chet shook his head. "O ye of little faith."

"Come on. Where'd you get the Vette? And those clothes?" Joe was growing impatient. He liked quick and easy solutions to any mystery.

Chet stepped away from the Vette, his arms opened wide. "This, my friends, is the true fruit of my labors." He pretended to pick lint from his new designer shirt. "And this is a little gift I allowed myself because I've done such a good job."

Frank finished his inspection of the car. "Come on, buddy. 'Fess up."

"Okay." Chet laughed. "Remember that job I told you about at the end of last semester?"

"The car-washing job?" Frank asked.

"Car-washing job?" Chet was disappointed and hurt. "No, the one selling used cars for my uncle Ed."

"You don't have an uncle Ed," Joe stated.

"Ed Brooke. He's been dad's friend since they were in high school, and he insists I call him Uncle Ed. He owns AutoHaus Emporium."

"That used-car joint in Southport?" Callie asked.

"Used-car joint?" Chet's chest fell again. "AutoHaus Emporium deals only in classic sports cars. Uncle Ed is the best salesman in the state, and I'm his assistant."

"Congratulations, Chet. This is really something," Frank said.

"Yeah," Joe chimed in. "Fantastic."

"Thanks," Chet replied, his face reddening with embarrassment. He really wasn't the show-off type, but he did want his friends to know that he had done well at something. "Since I posted the second highest sales for the past month, Uncle Ed gave me a bonus and is letting me drive this little baby around."

"Are you going to take us for a ride?" Callie asked.

Chet smiled. "Sure. But first—Mr. Pizza."

"I told you he wanted a free meal," Frank teased.

"Tonight, my friends, pizza, bread sticks, lasagna, whatever you want is on me," Chet announced.

"What?" Frank, Joe, and Callie exclaimed simultaneously. Chet rarely offered to buy one of them a meal, let alone treat all three of them.

"I told you Uncle Ed gave me a bonus along with my regular commission check and, well, let's just say that Chet Morton is doing *all right!*" Chet started around the Vette. "I'll meet you at Mr. Pizza. I want to park this baby in a safe area."

"Yeah," Joe said. "Wouldn't want it ripped off the first night, huh?"

Chet stopped cold. He shot Joe an angry look. "That's not very funny." He squeezed into the front seat, fired up the engine, and peeled away from the curb.

"I didn't mean anything by it," Joe hollered as Chet and the Vette disappeared down the ramp of the mall's underground parking garage.

Chet took a long time getting the car parked. By the time he joined the trio at their favorite Mr. Pizza booth, two supreme pizzas, three baskets of bread sticks, and two large pitchers of soft drinks cluttered the table.

"Hope you don't mind," Frank said, indicating the food. Chet slid in next to Callie.

"Listen, I didn't mean anything by that remark about the car being stolen," Joe apologized.

"Forget it," Chet said with a smile. He grabbed a slice of pizza, dumped ground peppers and Parmesan cheese on it, and took a big bite. "Southport has had several cars ripped off lately."

"Why?" Frank asked.

"So many cars have been stolen, especially the expensive imports and American sports cars, that the police think some dealers are ripping themselves off and then reselling the cars to foreign buyers overseas. The market in Japan is so good that even a low-priced classic that may sell for eight thousand dollars in the States goes for fifty thousand dollars over there."

Joe whistled.

"The police even questioned Uncle Ed."

"A conspiracy?" Frank asked.

"Yeah, can you believe it? If you knew Uncle Ed, you'd know he wouldn't cheat anyone. He's not like other used-car salesmen."

"How's that?" Frank asked.

"He's honest." Chet gulped down his soft

drink. "Well, who wants to be the first to go for a ride in the lean mean Chet machine?"

"Callie and I are going to the movies tonight," Frank said.

Joe smiled. "You two can go to the movies if you want, but I'm going cruising with my good buddy and his Vette."

"Right after I finish eating," Chet replied, as he and Joe high-fived each other.

After leaving Mr. Pizza, the foursome split up. Chet and Joe headed for the underground parking lot while Frank and Callie walked out to the van parked in the mall's spacious outdoor parking area.

Dusk was settling, and Frank turned on the headlights. He backed the van out of its parking space and headed for the exit.

"Watch out, Frank!" Callie shouted.

Someone had just run in front of the van. Frank slammed on the brakes, and the van screeched to a halt. He was getting ready to yell at the guy when he recognized—Chet!

The van's headlights lit both sides of Chet's face in an eerie white harshness that washed out all of Chet's features except his round eyes.

Chet looked like the walking dead.

Frank hopped from the van and darted to his friend. Before he could ask Chet what was wrong, Chet stumbled forward, his mouth trying to form words.

"It's gone," he gasped after several tense moments.

Frank shot him a puzzled look.

"The Vette's been stolen!"

Chapter

2

"ARE YOU SURE you didn't see a maroon Corvette drive out of here?" Joe asked the garage attendant.

"I told you I just came on duty ten minutes ago," the attendant answered angrily.

"Anything?" Frank asked as he joined Joe.

"No. He says he didn't see anything," Joe said, flipping a thumb at the attendant.

"You sure?" Frank asked the man in the booth.

"I told your pal here that I didn't see nothing," the attendant spat out.

"How about letting us check the time tickets?" Frank asked.

"Forget it, kid," he said, and sneered. "These tickets are the property of the Bayport

Mall Merchants Association, and you're not going to get your hands on them.''

Although he didn't want to, Joe turned and followed Frank to the van.

Chet was sitting in the chair behind the driver's seat, his face pale and sweaty. He questioned Joe with his eyes.

"Nothing," Joe replied. He slammed the door shut.

"What happened, Joe?" Callie asked as Frank steered the van out of the parking lot. "Chet won't say anything."

"We took the elevator down to the garage and the Vette was gone. Chet was like a madman running up and down the garage looking for the car." Joe frowned. "We're going to get that car back," Joe said with steel in his voice.

Frank glanced at his brother. He knew Joe like a book. Joe took personal offense whenever something happened to one of his friends, and he wouldn't stop at anything to solve this crime.

"We've got to report this to the police," Frank said. He turned the van onto Bayport's main street and steered it toward the Bayport police station.

"Can I help you kids with something?" asked a friendly voice as the foursome walked into the police station.

11

"Officer Riley!" Frank said, glad to see a friendly face. Officer Riley was an old friend who, while not approving of the Hardys' involvement in police matters, admired their accomplishments.

"Chet's car was stolen about an hour ago," Joe said.

"Who would want to steal that old clunker of yours?" Officer Riley asked Chet with a smile.

"Not *his* car," Frank explained. "A mint-condition classic Corvette."

The expression on Officer Riley's face became serious. He glanced at Chet once more but talked to Frank. "Let's use interrogation room one."

Once in the room, Chet explained why he was using the Corvette and all about his job at AutoHaus Emporium. Then he gave a detailed description of the Vette.

After scribbling down all the information provided by Chet, Officer Riley put his pencil on the table, looked Chet in the eye, and said, "You may not want to hear this, Chet, but I'm afraid you'll never see that car again."

"What?" Frank asked in disbelief.

"Chet's Vette is the third expensive sports car stolen in Bayport in the last two weeks," Officer Riley replied.

"What's that got to do with it?" Joe was growing angry.

Officer Riley leaned forward, his hands clasped together. "I don't know how I can put this gently, Chet, but your car is probably in a thousand little pieces headed to a thousand illegal parts houses."

Chet gasped.

The police veteran leaned back in his chair. "Ever hear of a 'chop shop'?"

"It's a garage where they dismantle stolen cars and then sell the parts," Frank replied.

"Exactly," Officer Riley confirmed.

"And you think Chet's car has been taken to a chop shop?" Callie asked.

"Yes." Officer Riley sighed.

"Why?" Callie asked.

"It's easier for the car thieves to sell a high-profile car like Chet's Corvette one piece at a time than to try to unload it intact," Joe explained.

Officer Riley nodded his head in agreement. "Plus the thieves actually make more money at it. The Vette would probably bring fifteen to seventeen thousand as is. Individual parts, however, are worth at least twenty-five thousand dollars. The fenders alone fetch three thousand apiece."

Chet groaned and put his head in his hands. "Uncle Ed'll kill me."

"I'm sorry, Chet," Riley said.

"What about finding the chop shop?" Joe asked.

"That's the problem. Southport's had a rash of thefts in the last six months, and it looks like the choppers are moving into Bayport."

"Choppers?" Callie asked.

"The guys who strip the cars, chop them up for resale as parts," Frank said.

Officer Riley rubbed his eyes and yawned. "So far, we haven't been able to link Bayport's thefts with Southport's so there's no coordination of investigations."

"Perhaps we can do something about that." Joe stood, ready for action.

"You kids stay out of this," Officer Riley warned. "Choppers aren't known for their good manners. They won't take kindly to you two trying to take away their livelihood." Officer Riley stood and opened the interrogation room door. "We're doing our best. Believe me, no one wants these choppers more than I do."

"Except Chet," Callie said solemnly.

Chet groaned.

They walked in silence to the Hardys' van and rode in silence to the Morton home. Chet politely refused several suggestions from the Hardys to go to the movies or the mall. Chet wouldn't say anything, only shake his head.

"He's really depressed," Frank said as he watched Chet slouch into his house.

"It wasn't his fault," Callie said. "He'll get over it."

"Let's hope so," Frank said.

The trio rode in silence once again.

Joe tried to come up with a plan that would help his buddy. But instead of thinking rationally, Joe became angry. By the time the Hardys reached home, Joe's anger had ignited into white heat.

"You two plan on moping around all day like you did all weekend?" Aunt Gertrude asked on Monday morning as she sipped her coffee in the Hardy kitchen.

After seeing Callie off on Saturday morning, Frank had tried to contact Chet, but Mrs. Morton explained that he had gone to Southport to tell his uncle Ed about the stolen Corvette. He thought he'd stay all weekend and work on Monday, too.

"We'll meet Chet when he gets off around five," Joe said, finishing off the last of the bacon. Then to Frank he said, "Maybe we ought to snoop around the repair and body shops here, see if we can pick up information about a chop shop."

"Good idea," Frank replied, pulling the van's keys from his pocket.

They were nearly out the door when the phone began ringing.

"I'll get it!" they shouted simultaneously, elbowing each other as they raced to the phone.

Aunt Gertrude beat both of them.

"Hello," she said, then listened intensely. "Excuse me? Who? Uncle Ed? We don't have an Uncle Ed—"

"It's for us, Aunt Gertrude," Frank said as he took the phone from her. "Thanks." He smiled. Aunt Gertrude disappeared. Frank put the phone to his ear. "Hello?"

"Is this Fenton Hardy?" Frank could tell the man on the other end was frightened, almost hysterical.

"No. This is Frank Hardy, his son."

"I need to talk to Fenton Hardy. *Please!* It's an emergency."

Frank could tell Joe was anxious to know about the phone call and punched the intercom button. "Mr. Hardy is out of town," Frank said.

"I must talk with Mr. Hardy!" the man sobbed. "My nephew, Chet Morton, has been kidnapped!"

Chapter

3

"KIDNAPPED?" JOE SHOUTED into the phone's intercom.

"I don't know. I'm not sure," Uncle Ed replied. His voice revealed that he was confused as well as terrified.

"Calm down, Mr. Brooke. What makes you think he's missing?" Joe asked quickly.

Mr. Brooke sighed. "Chet showed up at work Saturday morning and told me about the stolen Corvette. He felt so guilty. I told him it wasn't his fault. He's such a good kid. I've known him since he was—"

"What happened to Chet?" Frank interrupted.

"He felt he had to do something. I told him to let the police handle it. He's such a respon-

17

sible young man. Once, when he was younger, he broke an expensive—''

"*Chet*, Mr. Brooke," Joe said, controlling his impatience. "What happened to Chet?"

"Yes, I'm sorry. It's just that I'm so worried about him." Mr. Brooke paused. He took a deep breath.

Finally Mr. Brooke began. "Chet said the police all but closed the case on the Corvette, that it was probably stolen by some chop shop operators and was now in parts. He told me not to worry, that he would find the choppers and turn them over to the police. He left my office before I could stop him."

"What makes you think he's been kidnapped?" Frank asked.

"Chet called last night and said he had found two men he believes stole the Corvette. He was going to get the evidence and then call me this morning. But he never did. I did get a call from someone saying he had Chet this morning. That was all he said. I guess I'll get another call."

"Who were the two men?" Joe asked.

"A body shop owner named Butch Smith and a kid named John Drake."

"Did you call the police?" Frank asked.

"No, I can't do that." The man's voice reached a fevered pitch. "I know those two. They'll hurt Chet. Snake—he calls himself

Drake the Snake—used to wash cars for me. I fired him several months ago for stealing tools. Smith used to live in Southport about five years ago, and he just returned when he was paroled seven months ago.''

"He's an ex-con?" An awful thought crept to the forefront of Joe's mind and was soon confirmed by Mr. Brooke.

"Yes. Even before he went to prison, he had a nasty reputation. If he has Chet, he won't hesitate to hurt him if he thinks the police are involved. That's why I want to hire Mr. Hardy—to find Chet before Smith does something terrible to my nephew." He sobbed.

"Dad's out of town, Mr. Brooke, but Joe and I can handle the case," Frank said.

"No. *No!*" Uncle Ed shouted. "I don't want you boys involved. I feel bad enough about Chet and if you two get involved—"

"We've handled tough guys before," Joe interrupted. "Chet's our best friend. You can't expect us to just drop it."

A dead pause filled the air, the only noise the hissing of the phone line.

"Okay." Joe thought he heard a sob.

"Where can we find Smith and this Snake character?" Joe asked without hesitation.

"There it is," Frank said. He pulled the van into a parking lot stuck between a car wash and an old brick building. David's Den was hand-painted in bright Day-Glo orange on the faded white bricks.

Half the size of Bayport, Southport lay midway between New York City and the Hardys' hometown. The Hardys had been to Southport only a couple of times, but they knew the city well enough to find their way around.

Uncle Ed, as he insisted the Hardys call him, had explained that Snake could usually be found at David's Den, a pool hall and video arcade used as a hangout by Southport's more unsavory characters. He gave the Hardys a complete description of Snake. Frank decided that it would be best if he and his brother posed as car thieves and had Mr. Brooke get them a room at a motel.

"Hey, slow down," Frank shouted as Joe jumped from the van and all but ran toward the pool hall.

Joe stopped and placed his hands on his hips.

Frank ignored Joe's impatient stare. "We've got to play this slow and easy. You overact and Snake'll know we're not really car thieves."

Joe turned, and the Hardys strolled into David's Den.

Inside, they had to let their eyes adjust to the dimness of the pool hall. The large open room was crammed with pool tables. Video machines lined the walls. Each table had a single long fluorescent lamp hanging a couple of feet above it. Smoke and dust floated in the light and gave the place a dirty, sinister look.

The crack of pool balls bounced off the walls and sounded like rifle shots. Only half the tables were occupied, most by single players.

Joe sauntered toward a table and then over to a video machine. He dumped two quarters in one of the video machines and began playing the game. Frank leaned against the machine and scouted the room.

"See him?" Joe whispered.

"Not yet," Frank replied.

Without trying to look too obvious, Frank checked out the players. Toward the back of the room, almost hidden by the dimness of the room and the other players, was a figure who matched the description Ed Brooke had given them over the phone.

The young man looked to be six feet and weigh no more than 150 pounds. He wore a sleeveless T-shirt and ragged skintight jeans. Half of his thin, pinched face was covered by large teardrop sunglasses.

The young man leaned into the hazy fluorescent light—Frank *knew* he was their man. On Snake's left shoulder was a tattoo: a coiled rattlesnake, its mouth open wide, its fangs dripping with venom and blood. Below the snake, a curled banner proclaimed Born to Die, just as Uncle Ed had said there would be.

"He's in the back," Frank said.

Joe turned slightly and looked at Snake. He spotted the tattoo. "You're right. Let's do it."

They walked slowly from video game to video game, pretending to look at each one before moving on. When they reached the game closest to Snake's pool table, they stopped.

Snake was getting ready to fire the white cue ball down the length of the table toward the black number-eight ball that sat centered in front of a corner pocket. He hit the cue ball, and it rocketed down the table in a white blur. Frank grabbed the cue ball just before it could strike the eight ball.

"Hey, man!" Snake protested in a whiny voice. "That was a clean shot."

Frank knocked the eight ball into the hole with the cue ball and then dropped the cue ball into the pocket.

"Scratch, man. You lose," Frank said coldly.

"Hey!"

Joe stood next to Snake. "Your name Snake?" he asked, his tone menacing.

"Drake the Snake, man. Who wants to know?"

"Your new business partners," Frank replied.

"Wh-what?" Snake stammered.

"Outside," Joe hissed.

Snake gripped the cue stick with both hands, as if to swing it.

"I'll swat you like a fly," Joe growled.

"Hey, take it easy, Joe," Frank said. "Snake here doesn't want to cause any trouble." He smiled at the thin young man.

Snake threw the stick onto the table. "What do you two want?"

"Just to talk," Frank said, still smiling. "Could be some money in it for you."

"So? Talk." Snake sat on the table's edge.

"Out back," Joe ordered wtih a nod of his head.

Snake shrugged and headed toward the back door. Once in the alley, Snake turned and faced Joe with clenched fists.

Joe took a defensive karate stance. "Take your best shot."

"Hey, guys," Frank began as he moved between Joe and Snake, "is this any way to start off a partnership?"

"What partnership?" Snake asked, keeping his fists clenched, his eyes on Joe.

Frank elbowed Joe back a step. "You see, Snake, my brother and me got us a neat little gig in Bayport. So good in fact, that we don't need or want any outsiders interfering with our business."

"Hey, man, I don't even know you dudes," Snake cried.

Joe pounded and rubbed his knuckles into his left palm. "Someone's been ripping off cars in Bayport, *our* cars."

"What cars?" Snake's voice began to quiver.

"Expensive cars," Frank replied. "Like the neat little maroon Corvette we had our eyes on last Friday when someone boosted it. *You*."

"What about it?" Snake's voice cracked.

"We don't like creeps moving in on our territory." Joe made a grab for Snake, but was stopped by Frank.

"Take it easy, Joe. Snake seems to be a reasonable person." Frank winked at his younger brother. They had played the "good guy–bad guy" routine before and were good at it.

"Yeah?" Joe growled. "Well, I don't have time to mess around." He grabbed Snake's arm and stood toe to toe with Snake. "Stay out of our territory, understand?"

Frank was about to separate Joe from Snake, playing the good guy, when a gruff voice spoke up from behind them.

"Need some help, Snake?"

Frank and Joe spun around. An older man

stood just outside the rear door o;
hall, a steel blue .45 automatic at his sid

Joe let loose of Snake. Snake walked to
older man and stood behind him.

"They were going to kill me," he lied.

"Yeah?" replied the man. He raised the .45
straight out in front of him, chest level, and
cocked back the hammer. "Well, let's see if
we can't do something about that."

Chapter

4

THE ALLEY WAS too narrow and empty for Frank and Joe to jump to the side for cover. The end was several yards behind them.

"Kill us now, man, and you'll be passing up an opportunity to get rich," Frank said as calmly and casually as he could under the circumstances.

"Really?" the man said, chuckling.

"Blow 'em away, Butch," Snake ordered, a sudden bravado in his voice.

"Shut up, you wimp," Joe spit out at Snake, who shrank even farther behind Smith.

"Take his advice, Snake. It's a good thing I was coming in just as these two were taking you out the back door." Smith waved the .45 between Frank and Joe.

"I mean it," Frank continued. "We can make you a deal that you can retire on."

Smith hesitated, his eyes showing that he was interested. "Go on."

"I'm Frank Davis. This is my brother, Joe."

"Is that supposed to mean something?" Smith sounded bored.

"We know you boosted that Corvette in Bayport last Friday," Frank said.

Smith turned on Snake. "Been running your big mouth again, like you did to that Morton kid last night?"

Snake backed up, his hands raised. "N-n-no."

Frank and Joe exchanged knowing glances. Chet had found the right thieves.

"Yeah, he did," Frank called out, turning Smith's attention back to them. He decided to play a hunch. "You've hit our territory three times in the last two weeks."

Smith unlocked the hammer of the .45 and lowered it gently. *"Your* territory? I don't remember seeing any signs declaring Bayport a closed city."

"We've been boosting the hottest cars in Bayport for over a year," Frank said. "We've gotten used to the money. Your three heists the last couple of weeks have left our pockets a little empty."

"And we don't like it," Joe added.

"Just blow 'em away, Butch," Snake insisted.

"Shut up," Smith growled, and he elbowed Snake—hard.

Ed Brooke was right. Smith's temper was lightning quick and violent. The Hardys would have to be very careful.

Smith turned back to Frank and Joe, the .45 at his side.

"So. What's this plan that'll make me rich?"

"Not here," Frank said, chuckling. He nodded to Frank. "You come with me and Snake." He glared at Joe. "You follow. Try anything funny and Frankie here will eat a bullet."

"No problem, man," Joe said.

A few minutes later Frank and Joe stood in the middle of a large warehouse that had been converted into a makeshift garage. They both scanned the area, hoping to find a sign of Chet.

Along the walls were torches and welding tanks filled with oxygen and acetylene—gases that when combined made for a flame hot enough to melt the toughest metals, especially the steel used in cars. Air compressors, air drills, metal cutters, and socket wrenches completed the arrangement. Several vats large enough to hold fenders and engines sat at one end, fifty-gallon drums labeled Solvent sat next to them. By the smell, Frank could tell that the vats held an acid toxic enough to melt paint and burn down serial numbers.

Joe was disappointed that the Vette wasn't around. He did notice a makeshift office in a back corner of the warehouse. A good place to hide a kidnap victim. He nudged Frank and nodded toward the office.

"Cool place you have here," Joe said.

"It does the job," Smith replied. He sat on one of the drums. He pulled the .45 from his pants and pointed it at Frank. "Okay, smart guy. What's this plan?"

Frank tried to look unnerved. He crossed his arms and sighed.

"My brother and me have a sweet little thing going in Bayport. Plenty of rich kids driving expensive cars. The pickings are easy. The only problem is that we've had a hard time moving cars. No one wants to take a chance on buying a hot car in one piece."

"I still haven't heard anything to interest me enough to keep me from plugging you and your brother," Smith said.

Snake let loose with a loud cackle that echoed throughout the warehouse.

Joe curled one end of his lip and growled. Snake coughed and moved behind Smith.

Frank ignored the two. "Here's the deal. We can bring in more bread by chopping our cars.

The problem is we don't have the funds to start our own shop—"

"So you want to use my little business here," Smith interrupted.

"Exactly. We boost the cars from those Bayport brats, chop 'em here, and split the proceeds."

"And what do you figure would be a fair split?"

"Seventy-thirty."

Smith laughed loud and hard.

"What circus did you two clowns escape from?" He shook his head. "No way. I've got the shop, I got the equipment, I got my man Snake here who can boost any car, and I got it easy. Why should I take on two punks who just waltzed in off the street?"

"Because you're not a fool," Joe spoke up. "What my brother and me are offering you is too good to pass up, and you know it. Snake may be a good thief, but he's two cylinders short of full power. It won't be long until the Bayport police catch him and your little operation goes up—*kaboom!*" Joe made an exploding gesture with his hands.

"We know every little street and alley and escape route in Bayport," Frank added.

Smith sat silently, clutching and unclutching the .45 with nervous agitation. His expression was blank. Frank and Joe weren't sure what his reaction would be.

"You've got a point," he said after several tense moments. Smith stood, thrusting the .45 into his waistband. "Before we finalize this deal, you two have to pass a little test."

Frank smiled. "Name it," he said with confidence.

"Let's see how good you are. Joey here can stay and keep me and Snake company while you find a nice little expensive car to boost. Bring it back here without getting caught, and we'll see about finalizing the deal."

"That's all?" Frank asked.

"No. If you're not back here in fifteen minutes, I'll assume you got caught or can't do the job and Joey here—well, let's not think about that."

"I'm not going to be a hostage," Joe said angrily.

"Did I say anything about a hostage? You're just a little insurance to make sure your brother doesn't blow it." Smith tossed a small plastic black box to Frank. "Garage door opener," he explained. He glanced at his watch. "Now you've got fourteen minutes and twenty seconds."

"See you in ten," Frank smirked as he strutted through the door.

Once outside, Frank quickly walked several

blocks and then hailed a taxi. Two minutes later, he stepped from the taxi into the high-priced restaurant district of Southport, the parking lots bulging with expensive cars ranging from Cadillacs to Sterlings.

Frank knew the type of car that would best impress a chopper like Smith—a high-profile speedy sports car with high resale parts.

He casually crossed the street and entered a parking lot from the shadowy side of the restaurant, away from the parking valet who stood out in front of the driveway.

He strolled up to a midnight blue Porsche, using his peripheral vision to keep track of the valet and anybody else who might see him.

In a few seconds he was sitting in the Porsche's red leather front seat, its engine rumbling to life. He kept the lights off so as not to attract the valet's attention and slowly pulled the car out of its parking space. He guided the car toward the rear of the parking lot, away from the valet and traffic of the restaurant.

He let the car hop the curb and then gently accelerated forward. The last thing he wanted was to attract attention. This was no time to be stopped by the cops.

Suddenly the bright red and blue lights of a police cruiser filled the Porsche's small compartment. The ghostly cry of a police siren pierced the air.

Frank glanced at the speedometer to make sure he wasn't speeding. The dash was dark.

The lights! He had been so intent on going unnoticed that he had forgotten to turn on the lights once he had hit the brightly lit street.

He pulled on the light switch and mashed the accelerator to the floor. The Porsche jumped forward, and the rear wheels screamed as raw horsepower was unleashed.

In the rearview mirror, Frank could see the cruiser lurch forward, nudging closer to the Porsche. He shoved the gears into high and the smaller, swifter car soon outdistanced the police cruiser.

He pulled into an alley, and a second later slipped out onto a parallel street. He headed for the garage and was relieved to hear the police siren moving farther and farther away from him.

Joe sat on a rusty oil drum, avoiding the hard eye Smith was giving him. They said little to each other since Frank had left. Snake had whined, and Smith had ordered him to move a stack of tires to the other side of the garage.

Joe jumped as the warehouse suddenly echoed with a loud grating sound as the garage door began to rise. It had risen only four feet when a midnight blue Porsche burst through the narrow opening and screeched to a halt. Immediately, the garage door began to close again.

Frank jumped from the front seat, beaming with a big grin. He looked at his watch.

"Ten minutes and fifteen seconds exactly," he announced. He tossed the remote control to Smith.

Smith whistled. "Not a bad haul on such short notice." He paced around the Porsche. "I'm impressed, Frankie."

"You okay?" Frank asked Joe.

"Yeah. Just a little stiff," Joe replied. "We had a swell time." Noticing that Smith was distracted by the Porsche, Joe leaned closer to Frank and whispered, "You found it where Uncle Ed said it would be?"

Frank nodded and winked. They had anticipated that Smith would want some proof that he and Joe were honest-to-goodness car thieves, and what better way to prove this than to "steal" a car. Uncle Ed had willingly given up one of his finer cars in the hope that Chet would be found.

"You two staying somewhere?" Smith asked as he joined them.

"Yeah. The Southport Motor Inn," Frank replied.

"Good." He handed Frank another small black plastic box. "Here's a beeper. I'll call when I want you and Joey to make another hit.''

"I thought we passed the test," Frank protested.

"One test does not a partnership make. After all, I don't know if Joey knows the difference between a clutch and a steering wheel. But you, Frankie, are aces as far as I'm concerned."

"Okay," Frank said reluctantly. "Just one thing before we leave."

"What?"

"Don't call us Frankie and Joey again. Call us Frank and Joe or just call us Davis."

Smith's high-pitched roar of laughter echoed off the brick walls of the warehouse.

Half an hour later Frank and Joe "Davis" lumbered toward their second-floor room at the Southport Motor Inn. They were tired and worried. They had gained a foothold in Smith's operation, but they weren't any closer to finding Chet.

Frank unlocked the door and pushed his way into the darkness. Joe flipped on the light.

Then they froze.

A man sat in a chair across the room from the door. In one hand he held an open wallet. In the other he held a .357 magnum, its single barrel staring at Frank and Joe in deadly anticipation.

"Welcome home, Frank and Joe Davis. Or should I say Hardy? Whatever you two yahoos call yourselves, you're under arrest!"

Chapter

5

"WHAT ARE THE CHARGES, DETECTIVE?"
Frank asked, taking in the gold shield gleaming
from the man's open wallet.

The detective stood and put his wallet inside
his jacket. He held up his hand and began
counting. "Auto theft. Interfering with a police
investigation. Using a false name to register at
a motel." The detective snorted a laugh.

"Not funny," Frank said.

"It's a riot from where I'm standing."

Joe studied the short and balding detective
with the puffy eyes and massive bulldog jaw.
Not only did the man have bad manners, but
his clothing looked like Salvation Army re-
jects—matching dark green polyester jacket
and slacks, a food-stained paisley print blue
tie, and an orange double knit shirt. His walrus

mustache held the crumbs of what had probably been his dinner.

"Just who are you?" Joe asked.

The man straightened up, a hard look crossing his face. "I'm Detective-Sergeant Terry Cronkite, head of Southport's Auto Theft Division."

"So? What do you want with us?" Joe asked.

Cronkite shifted his cold, hard stare to Joe. "I'll tell you what I want from you, wise guy. I want you out of Southport in the next fifteen minutes or I'm booking you into our finest accommodations."

"How did you know our names and where we were?" Frank asked.

"I get a call last Saturday from Ed Brooke wanting to file a stolen car report. So, I file it. I return this afternoon for more information, and I find Mr. Brooke climbing the walls with worry because his nephew tried to play cop," Cronkite said. He put his pistol in its shoulder holster. "I trust you two won't do anything foolish."

"Just finish your story," Joe said.

Cronkite shrugged. "Anyway, I finally get Mr. Brooke calmed down, and he not only tells me that he thinks this nephew of his—a, uh, Chet Morgan—"

"*Morton*," Joe said through clenched teeth.

"And he's not his real nephew. Mr. Brooke is an old family friend."

"Yeah. Right." Cronkite took a stick of gum from his pocket, unwrapped it, and put it in his mouth. "Not only is this Morton kid missing, to make matters worse, you two yahoos talk Mr. Brooke into letting you 'pretend' to steal a car for the very people who may have kidnapped Morton!"

Cronkite rubbed the back of his neck and sighed. He looked from Frank to Joe.

"And you know what happened to that thirty-five-thousand-dollar car you so politely delivered to Smith and that numbskull assistant of his? They chopped it!" He blew and popped a small bubble.

"Real comedian, aren't you?" Joe said.

Cronkite's face turned crimson.

"Listen, punk. The only reason you and your brother aren't in jail now is because Brooke is a friend of mine and he's worried sick about his nephew. He doesn't need any junior detectives from Bayport botching up my case."

"We're not 'junior detectives,' *Detective*," Frank insisted. "We want to find Chet as much if not more than you do. He's our best friend. We've known him all our lives."

Cronkite's breathing was hard. He continued to stare at Joe, who glared back at him. He glanced at Frank, then returned to Joe. He pulled on his mustache.

"Yeah. That's what Brooke said."

Frank was relieved to see some calm return to Cronkite's face.

"I'm sure you two don't mean any real harm," Cronkite continued, "but this is out of your league. We're talking major serious here."

"We know that. We wanted Uncle Ed, uh, Mr. Brooke, to call the police, but he was afraid that Smith would harm Chet if the police were involved. We were going to contact you in the morning."

"We can help you on this one, Detective," Joe added.

"Uh-uh, no way," Cronkite asserted with a wave of his hand. "That's all I need in my file, that I let a couple of crazy kids from Bayport assist in a police investigation."

"We're not kids," Joe said.

"You know Officer Con Riley in Bayport?" Frank asked.

"Con? Sure. What about him?"

"Call him. He'll square with you that Joe and I are legit, that we know what we're doing."

"Didn't you two hear me? You're not a part of this case, you're through. Period."

"Then arrest us," Joe insisted.

"What?"

Joe stood directly in front of Cronkite. "The way I see it, you're going to have to either arrest us or let us help in some way. We're not returning to Bayport without our friend."

A heavy burden seemed to weigh on Cronkite's shoulders. He sighed, then threw his hands into the air.

"All right. I'll phone Con. But that doesn't mean I'm going to open the doors and welcome you yahoos with outstretched arms. I ought to call your bluff and let you spend some time in a Southport holding cell with the other derelicts."

Cronkite shook his head and reached for the phone.

Frank motioned Joe over to the opposite side of the room while Cronkite made his call.

"We've got to convince him that he can't do without us," Frank whispered to Joe.

"Got any ideas?"

"Yes," Frank answered.

Minutes later, Cronkite hung up the phone.

"You boys have quite a rep for putting bad guys away. I'm impressed."

"Good," Joe said, excited. "What do you want us to do?"

"Whoa, cowboy! I didn't say I wanted you two to do anything," Cronkite said, his hands raised. "I just said I was impressed. You may have Con convinced that you're a pair of heroes, but to me you're still two kids interfering in a police investigation."

"Why haven't you busted Smith's operation before now?" Frank asked. "You obviously know he's chopping cars."

"Smith is just the icing. We want the whole cake—the fencer, the guy who's actually moving the parts. So far we haven't been able to get anyone undercover to find out who that is."

Frank rubbed his chin. He looked at Joe, winked, and smiled, then back at Cronkite.

Innocently, he asked, "You mean that in several months of investigation by the Southport Auto Theft Division you haven't been able to accomplish what two junior detectives from Bayport did in a couple of hours?"

Cronkite's bulldog jaw dropped. "I—I—I . . ."

Frank could tell Joe was stifling a laugh, and he, too, had to control himself.

"How much longer is it going to take before you get someone on the inside as deep as Joe and I are right now? But that isn't our concern, is it, Joe?" Following Frank's lead, Joe shook his head. "Joe and I have to get back to Bayport, tell Officer Riley how his old buddy passed up an opportunity to shut down one of the biggest chop shop operations in the area. Let's split, Joe.''

They headed for the door. Frank held his breath, hoping his bluff would work.

"Hey, wait a minute." Cronkite nervously laughed and put himself between the Hardys and the door. "I didn't say you couldn't help somehow. I just needed to be sure, that's all."

Neither Frank nor Joe returned the detective's plastic smile.

Cronkite stared at them for a few seconds, sighed, then raised a finger. "Rule Number One: I'm in charge and you follow my orders. Rule Number Two: When in doubt, refer to Rule Number One. Do we understand each other?"

"Clearly," Frank said.

"All we want to do is find our friend," Joe added.

"Okay," Cronkite replied without hesitation. "How is Smith going to contact you if he needs you?"

Frank pulled the beeper from his belt and held it up.

"These modern horse thieves have it easy," Cronkite said, back to his cynical self. "I've got an undercover officer who hasn't been able to get on the inside of Smith's gang yet." Cronkite paused. "Emerson Sauter. A rookie, but a good cop."

"A rookie?" Frank couldn't believe it.

"I wouldn't be choosy about my partners, young man," Cronkite replied, one eyebrow cocked. "Officer Sauter was especially chosen for this assignment. You'll find out why tomorrow. Know where Royce's Garage is located?"

"We can find it," Joe said.

"That's right—you're 'detectives.' Report to the officer for further instructions at oh-nine-hundred hours, sharp!"

"Does he use an undercover name?" Frank asked.

"He?" Then Cronkite laughed. "Oh, no, *he* uses *his* real name."

Frank wondered what Cronkite thought was so funny, but dismissed it as part of the detective's strange sense of humor.

"You'd better introduce us by our aliases," Frank advised.

Cronkite nodded as he opened the door. "I still can't believe I'm putting my career into the hands of a couple of junior detectives from Bayport. What a world!"

After a fitful night's rest, the Hardys were up early, heading for Royce's Garage on the other side of Southport. The hotcakes they had ordered for breakfast had been cold and doughy, and Joe was irritable.

Joe turned the van into the driveway of a

run-down building sitting far back off the main road. Various car parts littered most of the driveway. ROYCE'S GARAGE was painted across the large front window.

Joe had to jockey the van around the trash.

"This is it? This is the big undercover operation?" Joe stared in disbelief.

Frank sat up. "Looks more like a war zone than a repair shop."

"I don't think they put a lot of money or planning into this," Joe said with a groan.

"Let's meet this Sauter character and see what he has to say for himself."

Because the bay doors were shut, Frank and Joe walked into the garage's outer office. Joe tried an inner office door, but it was locked.

The walls of the outer office were cluttered with hot-rod posters and personal photographs. Joe checked out several of the photos. Many were of a pretty girl and classic fifties cars. The girl looked about seventeen or eighteen, her long red hair framing a beautiful face and green eyes. Joe fell in love immediately.

"Out here," Frank said. "There's a mechanic under a car in one of the bays."

"Officer Sauter?" Joe asked as they approached the mechanic.

No answer. They knew he wasn't asleep; they could hear him tinkering under the car.

"Officer Sauter," Frank called out. "It's

Frank and Joe Davis. Detective Cronkite called you last night about us.''

Still no answer.

''Rudeness seems to be this police department's primary attitude,'' Joe quipped. ''Hey!'' he shouted as he kicked the greasy boots of the mechanic.

The mechanic yelled and whipped out from under the car on the wheeled crawler, leaping up with lightning speed.

Instinctively, Joe cocked his fist to protect himself. He pulled his punch when he saw that the mechanic was a girl.

What Joe didn't realize soon enough was that she had flung a heavy pipe wrench straight at his head!

Chapter
6

"LOOK OUT!" Frank shouted as he shoved Joe aside.

The heavy pipe wrench bounced on the floor.

Joe cocked his fist, ready to punch the mechanic.

"Try it, jerk, and you'll end up eating concrete," the mechanic threatened in a soft but stern tone.

Joe stared at the mechanic. She was in a defensive karate stance, posed to strike, her baseball cap turned around backward.

"Come on, macho man," the young woman challenged. "You started this—let's see if you can finish it."

"Wait a minute," Joe protested, his hands raised. "I'm not going to fight a girl."

The young woman's green eyes flared. "My gender has nothing to do with this. I'll use you to mop up this floor."

"What's your problem?" Joe looked to Frank for help, but Frank only seemed amused by his younger brother's predicament.

"I'll tell you what my problem is," the young woman said slowly. "I just spent the better part of two hours making delicate adjustments to this car's transmission, and your little kick caused me to slip and knock it all out of whack. That's my problem!" The woman pulled a rag from the rear pocket of her coveralls and began wiping red transmission fluid from her hands. "But I guess an ape like you wouldn't know about such things."

"Wait a minute," Joe began. He glanced at the name stitched over the coveralls's pocket— Emmy. Emmy? *Emerson* Sauter? You're a mechanic? I mean, you're a woman?"

"I'm a cop, too. Got a problem with that? You two from Cronkite?"

"Yes," Frank said, trying not to smile.

"Look, if I'd known you were a woman, I wouldn't have kicked you," Joe explained. He turned to Frank. "Whoever heard of a girl named Emerson?"

Emmy took off her cap, and her red hair fell to her shoulders. The girl in the photos, Joe realized.

"It just so happens," Emmy finally replied, "that my father named me after Emerson Fittipaldi, the Brazilian race car driver. Not that it's any of your business."

"Look, we're sorry," Frank apologized, stepping between Emmy and Joe. "I'm Frank Davis. You've already met Joe." Frank stuck out his hand, and Emmy shook it firmly. "Did Cronkite tell you about us?"

Emmy stomped over to a large stainless-steel sink and began washing the grease from her face and hands.

"Yes. And I'll tell you both right now, I don't like this arrangement. The last thing I need to do is baby-sit a couple of teenagers."

"Don't worry about us," Joe said.

"I *have* to worry about you. My life may depend on it." Emmy towel dried her hands. "Let me tell you two this." She was addressing Joe more than she was Frank. "Cronkite has given me full discretion in this case. What I say goes."

Frank's beeper sounded in a rapid series of staccato chirps, and all three jumped.

"What's that?" Emmy asked, distrust in her voice and eyes.

"Smith," Frank explained. He shut off the beeper.

"I'll call and find out what he wants," Joe volunteered.

"Phone's on the desk," Emmy shouted after Joe. She threw the garage bay door open and stepped outside.

"Cronkite should have told us a little more about you," Frank said.

"Why? Would you have objected to working with a woman?" Emmy leaned against a sleek red and black fastback coupe.

"No. And don't be so defensive." Frank suddenly realized why he was beginning to like this rookie cop—she reminded him of Callie. The same sparring with Joe, the same quick temper, the same pretty face.

Emmy shifted. "Sorry."

"I know we haven't started out on the right footing. Let's begin again." Frank straightened to his full height. He stuck out his hand. "Hi. I'm Frank Davis, undercover car thief and all-around good guy."

Emmy stared for a moment, then laughed. She grabbed Frank's hand and shook it. "Hi, Frank. I'm Emerson Sauter, *your boss*."

They both laughed.

Joe was annoyed as he joined them outside. He didn't see anything funny.

"The final test," he said to Frank, ignoring Emmy.

"Test?" Emmy asked.

"We're not full members of Smith's little club yet," Frank explained. "We've got to boost one more car and then he'll make us full partners."

"Not 'we,'" Joe said. "Me. Smith wants me to prove I can pull off a job in broad day light."

"I don't think it's smart for you two to be stealing cars," Emmy said flatly.

"Got it covered," Joe said. "I called Uncle Ed, and he's lending us his own car to rip off. A brand-new Cadillac."

"Wow!" Emmy exclaimed.

"Uncle Ed's willing to give up his dealership to get Chet back," Joe replied. To Frank he said, "I'll need you to drop me off at Smith's."

"No, wait," Emmy spoke up as they headed for the van. "Joe, you take the van to Smith's. Frank, help me check out a salvage yard I think is fencing Smith's chopped parts."

"Okay with me," Frank replied to Joe's questioning glance.

Joe didn't like the idea of being separated, and he didn't like being bossed around by a woman.

"All right. I'll meet you back at the motel." With that, Joe hopped in the van and peeled out of the driveway, dodging various piles of junk.

"A real hothead," Emmy said.

"He's just anxious to find Chet. So am I," Frank replied.

"I don't blame you. I know what it's like to have someone you love taken away from you so suddenly, so violently."

Frank was startled by the faraway, painful tone in Emmy's voice. He was ready to ask her about it when she turned and walked toward the office.

"I've got to change. You wait in the car."

They headed out of Southport on a road that led into the country. Emmy had slipped into faded blue jeans and an old bowling shirt with Royce's Gear Heads and Gutter Balls embroidered on the back, and a bowling ball smashing into a set of pistons.

"I'm sorry if I seemed so defensive back at the garage," Emmy said. "I suppose it irks me just knowing you two have gotten into Smith's gang when I've been trying for six months."

"Beginner's luck," Frank said.

"Not from what Cronkite told me about you two."

Frank didn't know why, but he was embarrassed. In many ways, Emmy *was* a lot like Callie.

"Where are we going?" Frank asked.

"Paradise Salvage," Emmy replied. "Although I haven't been able to prove it, I think Max Elburk is moving chopped parts through his salvage hotline."

"Salvage hotline?"

"Nearly all the salvage yards across the nation are linked by a special computer hotline. If someone comes in needing a special part and a salvage yard doesn't have it, a manager gets on the modem with his fellow junkers. In a matter of minutes, he has the part ordered and shipped from one of his buddies' salvage yards."

"I didn't realize junkyards were so high tech."

"To you they may be junkyards, Frank, but those rusting old heaps of wrecked cars are lined with pure gold."

Emmy turned off the paved highway and onto a dirt road, dust flying into the air.

A large two-story barn sat on the edge of the front section of the salvage yard. The barn was dotted with orange and pink and purple and yellow painted flowers. Large white peace symbols from the sixties danced between the flowers. A wooden sign painted in bright pink letters announced Paradise Salvage.

Emmy laughed at Frank's stunned expression.

"Did I forget to tell you that Max Elburk is a little strange?" she asked as she parked the car.

"How strange?"

"*Strange*," Emmy replied. "All we have in

the files is that Max Elburk once designed computer software, and then about a year ago, he got fed up with his suits and ties and oxford shoes. He bought this salvage yard, grew his hair long, and started chanting and meditating."

"Chanting?" Frank asked, stepping from the car.

"He claims it calms him down, puts him in touch with the 'universal soul.' "

They stepped into the front office, which was at the front of a house. Emmy hit the bell on the counter several times, its ring echoing off the walls.

"What's that?" Frank asked, alarmed.

From somewhere behind the house came a steady, persistent humming and crunching.

"That's Max's crusher," Emmy replied. "It flattens cars into thin steel wafers or squeezes them into metal squares."

Moments later Max Elburk burst through the beaded curtain that separated the office from the rest of the house.

Emmy hadn't exaggerated Elburk's appearance. Frank had to keep from snickering at the middle-aged hippie.

Elburk's long, stringy gray hair reached his shoulders. Wire-rimmed glasses that were tinted purple sat perched on his thin nose and contrasted with his orange and yellow tie-dyed T-shirt.

"Emmy! I thought I heard someone. I was in back, chanting. How you doing?" Max Elburk drawled.

"Great," Emmy replied. "How about yourself?"

"I feel better now."

"Hope we didn't interrupt your meditating," Frank said.

Elburk shot a questioning glance at Emmy.

"This is Frank Davis, an old friend. Frank, this is Max Elburk."

Frank stuck out his hand. "Good to meet you."

"Pleasure," Elburk said, slapping Frank's hand instead of shaking it.

Emmy smiled and said, "Hey, Max, I'm replacing a tranny on a Vette, and I need a plate that isn't cracked or burned. Got one on hand?"

"Uh, don't think so," Elburk said slowly, his forehead wrinkled in thought.

Frank was impressed with Emmy's knowledge of mechanic slang. A tranny was a transmission. A plate was a clutch plate. He was beginning to understand why Cronkite had selected this particular rookie for the chop shop undercover operation.

"You sure?" Emmy pleaded. "I really need

it. I need to have the Vette finished by this afternoon. I could look in the parts barn if you're too busy.''

"No, no, that's okay. I'll check it out for you. If I don't have it there, maybe I can get it over the wire." Elburk disappeared through the beaded curtains.

"We may be out of luck, Frank," she said after Elburk had left.

"Why?"

"Chet's car was a Vette, right?"

"Right."

"I was hoping that if Smith was using Max to fence his chopped parts that—"

"Perhaps Smith brought the parts from Chet's car here," Frank finished.

"You're a fast learner, you know that?" Emmy's green eyes showed admiration for Frank.

Frank felt himself blush.

"However," Emmy said, "either he's holding out or he just doesn't have any. Which means he may not be fencing Smith's parts for him."

"If he is fencing for Smith, he may know where Chet is."

"Maybe." Emmy sighed. She walked over to a battered couch, sat down, grabbed a well-worn hot-rod magazine, and flipped through the pages. "This may take a while."

Frank leaned against the counter. He didn't like standing around while his best friend was in danger.

Frank decided to look around Elburk's house. He knew Emmy wouldn't like the idea, so he slowly walked backward, hoping not to distract her attention away from her magazine. He glanced through the beaded curtains and silently slipped through the opening.

He thought he was safe inside when he heard a pair of menacing growls. He turned his eyes to his right. Just inside were two massive black mastiffs crouched in an attack stance, their black lips pulled back over large, sharp yellow teeth. Frank knew that one move on his part would be excuse enough for the dogs to attack.

"Now what are you going to do, *Detective?*" asked Emmy somewhere behind Frank. Frank heard the beaded curtain rustle. Emmy stood beside him. Frank could see she had her arms folded and stood casually, as though nothing was wrong. "Believe it or not, their names are Peace and Love. They'll attack you, all right, unless you're properly introduced to them. Peace! Love! *Take it easy!*"

To Frank's surprise, the dogs relaxed, wagged their tails, and bounced over to Emmy, who knelt down and rubbed their heads.

Frank took a long-awaited breath. "You three act like you're old friends."

"I've been out here so often looking for old car parts that we've gotten to know each other quite well." Emmy stood. "And now, Frank Davis, I'd like to introduce you to Peace and Love. Boys, meet Frank Davis."

The two mastiffs looked at Frank, their heads turning from side to side.

"Go ahead, Frank. As long as you know the heel command, they're harmless."

Frank slowly stretched out his hands and patted the dogs on their heads. The dogs wagged their tails and tried to lick Frank's hands.

"I knew you three would make good friends." Emmy turned and walked back into the office, leaving Frank alone with the dogs. Frank glanced at the dogs and quickly followed.

Max was just coming through the front door as Frank entered the office.

"Oh—Max," Emmy said, covering for Frank. "I was just showing Frank your sixties record collection."

Max eyed Emmy.

"Yeah," Frank said. "You've got some cool old albums." Frank noticed that Max's T-shirt and jeans were now dirty, his face sweaty, and his hands greasy.

"Sorry, babe," Max said as he walked around the counter. "No such thing. I'll put a request out over the hotline. Want me to call you later?''

''Yeah, I guess.'' Emmy sighed. Her hunch hadn't panned out. ''Come on, Frank.''

''Be cool, you two,'' Max said with a cheerful wave.

''That's that,'' Emmy blurted out as she peeled away from Paradise Salvage.

''Maybe he was just playing it cool,'' Frank said to console Emmy. ''A Vette is stolen and chopped Friday night. You come looking for Vette parts Tuesday. Max may be a little weird, but he doesn't seem stupid.''

''Maybe you're right.''

The fastback suddenly leapt forward in a burst of speed, pressing Frank back against his seat.

''Hey!'' Frank shouted. ''Slow down!'' His eyes widened as they neared the paved intersection.

''I can't,'' Emmy yelled. ''The pedal's stuck.''

Frank watched as Emmy tried to pull the pedal up with her foot. It wouldn't budge. The car was approaching the intersection at ninety miles per hour.

Emmy pounced on the brakes with both feet. The car jerked as it slowed down, but sped up again as the brake pedal sank to the floor.

''Brakes are gone!'' Emmy shouted.

The intersection loomed before them like a black ribbon of death.

Emmy stomped on the emergency brake pedal. Nothing happened.

"Look out!" Frank shouted.

Emmy swerved the car to the left to avoid a semitractor trailer. The car fishtailed out of control. Emmy did gain control just as they were headed for a narrow bridge.

"Get the ignition, Frank!" Emmy yelled.

Frank knew what Emmy wanted him to do. By shutting off the engine, the power would be cut off, and the car would eventually slow down. Emmy couldn't do it: She needed both hands on the steering wheel to control the rampaging car.

He stripped off his shoulder seat belt, reached over, and shut off the engine, quickly flipping the ignition switch backward to accessory so the steering wheel wouldn't lock.

The high-pitched roar of the car's runaway engine died, and the fastback became strangely silent.

Emmy gasped. Frank followed her terrified gaze. They were approaching one of the small bridge's concrete pillars at ninety miles per hour!

Chapter

7

"WATCH THIS, BUDDY BOY," Snake said.

Joe sighed. For the umpteenth time, he watched as Snake flipped a peanut high into the air and caught it in his mouth.

Smith had insisted that Snake accompany Joe to grade him on his performance. Joe soon decided that he would have preferred the company of real rattlesnakes to this twit.

"Real neat," Joe sneered. "Know any disappearing tricks?"

Snake thought for a moment, his brow knitted in thought. "No." He shrugged. "Sorry, Joe."

Joe took a breath that whistled through gritted teeth.

They had walked around Southport for almost an hour. Snake had wanted to steal another Porsche, and Joe had had to explain to him that the cops would be keeping an eye out for two teenagers riding around in such an expensive car, especially a freaky-looking teenager like Snake. Snake took Joe's sarcastic remark as a compliment.

Uncle Ed had yet to deliver the Caddy to the prearranged "steal" site. If he didn't show soon, Joe would really have to steal a car just to keep Snake from getting suspicious.

A queasy feeling settled like a rock in Joe's stomach.

"Come on," Joe ordered. "Let's head down Third and see what's happening there."

They rounded a corner single-file, and Joe came to an abrupt halt as he spotted Uncle Ed several yards away, heading straight for him. Snake didn't have time to stop and ran into the back of Joe.

"Hey," Snake protested, the bag of peanuts hitting the pavement.

Joe fired a look at Uncle Ed. He jerked his head to the side. A puzzled, questioning expression creased Uncle Ed's face. Joe nodded to the side again. A sudden understanding crossed Uncle Ed's face, and he disappeared into a nearby shop.

"I think we just found our car," Joe announced.

"Really? Where?" Snake asked.

"That sports Caddy over there."

"Cool," Snake replied.

"Check the area," Joe ordered.

They strolled across the street. Joe became annoyed and angry. Snake looked too casual, walked too calmly. They would be caught for sure.

"Do it, Joe," Snake said as they reached the car.

In a split second, Joe had the driver's door open and was in the front seat, leaning over to unlock Snake's door.

"Uh-oh," Snake groaned.

Joe had spotted the steering wheel locking clamp at the same time Snake had. Without hesitation, he busted the clamp's lock and had the Cadillac's engine purring.

"Cool," Snake said.

Joe pulled out onto the street.

"Three seconds!" Snake shouted.

Joe jumped in his seat. "What's wrong?"

"It took only three seconds to boost this Caddy. You know what kind of bread we'll make for chopping this baby? Over thirty grand a second. Man, that beats minimum wage." Snake flipped on the stereo, tuned in a heavy metal station, and turned up the volume to an ear-shattering scream.

Joe just as quickly switched off the radio.

"What's your problem, man?" Snake spit out in his first real defiance toward Joe.

Joe stomped on the brake as they approached a red light. Snake slid forward, his head hitting the padded leather dash with a thud, his sunglasses flying onto the floor.

"Ooooow! What do you think you're doing?" Snake growled.

"We don't need to draw attention to ourselves. Just play it cool and celebrate *after* we get the Caddy to the garage," Joe said.

"Okay, man," Snake groaned, putting his sunglasses back on. "That's cool." Snake leaned back and began hissing a song through his teeth.

Joe shook his head and eased the Cadillac through the intersection. Frank had been right. Snake was not only slow, he was a finalist for Pinhead of the Year.

They were several blocks from the garage and Joe was starting to feel a little easier when Snake bolted up and shouted, "All right!"

Startled, Joe looked around, expecting to see a cop somewhere nearby.

"Will you look at that," Snake said, pointing.

Joe followed Snake's gaze to a small red two-seat sports convertible several feet ahead of them. He glowered at Snake. "So?"

"That's the hottest American sports car

made," Snake proclaimed. "It's worth two of these Caddies."

Joe's temples pulsed as he sensed the meaning behind Snake's statement. "We've got our quota for the day."

"You and that hotshot brother of yours ever play 'bump-and-rob'?" Snake's face was alive with excitement.

"No," Joe said quickly.

"It's simple. What's the biggest mistake people make when they have a little fender bender? I'll tell you," Snake said without waiting for Joe and whispered as if he were revealing a deep, dark secret. "They leave their keys in the ignition when they get out to inspect the damage."

"Forget it," Joe shot back.

"Man, this is perfect. No traffic. The driver's an old woman."

"I said forget it!"

"Okay, Joe. Okay."

Snake leaned back in his seat. Then without warning, Snake stepped on Joe's foot, mashing the accelerator to the floor. The Cadillac jerked forward. Joe slammed on the brakes, but not before the Cadillac clipped the rear end of the woman's car.

"All right!" Snake cheered. He jumped from the car before Joe could protest. "Wait for my signal, man, and then haul out of here."

Joe tried in vain to grab Snake and pull him back into the car.

"Hey, what's your problem, lady?" Snake yelled at the woman as she scampered back to the rear of her car.

"Oh, dear me. Oh, my," she cried out, confusion and fear in her voice.

Joe was surprised to see such an old woman driving an expensive sports car. She was dressed as though she were having tea with her bridge club. She wrung her hands and looked helpless as Snake continued to yell at her.

She reminded Joe of Aunt Gertrude.

"When's the last time you had those brake lights checked, huh?" Snake yelled at her.

"Well, I, oh my," the woman whimpered.

"Where'd you get your license? A convenience store?"

Joe had heard enough. He got out of the car. He'd get Snake back into the Cadillac if he had to break the creep's neck doing it.

Just as Joe stepped toward the woman, Snake yelled out, "Now!" shoved the old woman to the ground, and jumped into the woman's car. He fired up the engine and with a loud cackle and wave, peeled way.

Joe reached down to help the woman up, but she slapped his hands away.

She slowly got up and stared at Joe, her face

grief-stricken. She looked at Joe with hate in her eyes.

Then she screamed, "Thief! Thief!"

The old woman sobbed and covered her face.

Despite his desire to help the woman, he had to leave quickly before a crowd gathered. If caught, Cronkite wouldn't hesitate to charge him with auto theft and assault-and-battery and anything else the crusty detective could invent. As soon as he could, he'd call the police and tell them about the stolen car, but he'd do it anonymously.

Joe jumped back into the Cadillac, gently guided it around the woman, and sped away.

A cold, sharp metallic claw gripped Joe's spine. He shuddered at the image of the woman's dark, hateful stare.

For the first time in his life, Joe Hardy felt like a genuine thief.

Chapter

8

FRANK HAD TO SLOW the car down quickly or they'd disintegrate when they hit the concrete pillar.

He grabbed the column shift lever and slammed the transmission into reverse. He was using the transmission's reverse gear as a brake. The gears crunched like some metallic monster devouring a scrap-iron victim.

It took all of Frank's strength to hold the shift lever in the reverse position. They were still approaching the bridge and the concrete pillar at over seventy miles per hour.

Keeping one hand on the shift lever, Frank grabbed the steering wheel and twisted it slightly to the left.

The car glanced off the side of the pillar and shot onto the bridge. It caromed from one side of the bridge to the other, slamming into concrete-and-steel pillars with piercing metallic screams.

Sparks and razor-sharp concrete splinters flew into the windows like angry darts and hit Emmy and Frank in the face and arms.

Frank tried to keep the wheel straight. If they could make it across the bridge, they had a good chance of running the car into a field, where it could get bogged down in dirt and high grass.

The car slammed into a pillar, bounced off like a rubber ball, spun several times, and came to an abrupt stop.

Frank's head hit the steering wheel, dazing him. He leaned back in his seat and tried to focus on the car's windshield. A multitude of spiderwebs spread out across the glass. The shatterproof glass must have been hit by the flying concrete, creating the spiderweb effect.

Something warm trickled down his forehead. His vision was blurred by a red haze. Blood!

Emmy gasped.

Frank was suddenly aware of a new and immediate danger.

The car had indeed stopped. It had smashed through one of the bridge's aluminum railings and sat teetering above a dry, rocky riverbed fifty feet below. Every move that Emmy and Frank made, no matter how slight, caused the car to seesaw and inch closer toward the fifty-foot drop.

"Don't move," Frank warned. He took a deep breath to help clear his throbbing head. Seconds passed like minutes.

"All right," he finally said. "Move when I do, as I do, and when I tell you to."

He steadied his breathing and fought off visions of Emmy and him and the car sliding off the bridge and smashing onto the rocks below.

"Put your left hand on the door handle."

Emmy watched Frank from the corner of her eye.

"Pull the handle up slowly. *Easy!*"

Like twin reflections in a mirror, Frank and Emmy moved together. The inner latches of the two door locks clicked simultaneously.

A screeching metallic squeal shattered the air as the car lurched over the edge of the bridge.

"Frank!" Emmy cried out.

"Now!" Frank yelled.

Frank slammed his shoulder into his door and in one smooth motion threw himself free of the falling car. He hit the asphalt pavement hard and rolled clear.

Crumbled concrete kicked into the air as the car slid forward, as if in slow motion, and rolled off the edge of the bridge. Frank shuddered when he heard the crunch of the car as it slammed into the rocks of the dry riverbed.

"You okay, Emmy?" Frank stood. He blinked and rubbed his eyes in disbelief.

"Yeah," she wheezed. "I think so." She smiled.

Frank stood up and placed his hands behind his head to relieve the pressure on his lungs and rib cage. He felt as if he had just finished a marathon race with death.

Emmy stood up slowly. "I'm just glad these back roads are so deserted," she said.

"Yeah, aren't we lucky?" Frank said sarcastically.

"Let's hitch back to town and get cleaned up before I try to explain to Cronkite why his car is in the bottom of a dry riverbed."

"Cronkite's car?" Frank would have shouted if his chest didn't hurt so much.

"He dropped it off just before you two arrived. He wanted me to drive a newer car."

They had walked less than a mile when an old man driving a battered pickup loaded with paint and painting equipment in the truck bed offered them a ride.

"Watch where you sit," Emmy warned Frank as they climbed into the open back.

Frank didn't have time to heed Emmy's warning. The pickup lurched forward and

Frank sat squarely in a paint tray still wet with pink paint.

Emmy giggled. Then she chuckled. Soon, she was laughing so hard, she was crying.

Frank tried to look angry with a deep frown. Then he burst out laughing, too.

"I don't know what's so funny," Frank said with a sigh. "We may have escaped back there, but we've got to face Cronkite now."

"Yeah, I can't wait to see the look on that square face of his when I tell him his car is now a compact." Emmy let loose with another barrage of laughter, holding her sides.

Frank joined her. In the truck's rearview mirror, he could see the old man glance at them as if they were crazy.

"What do you think happened?" Frank asked after several moments.

Emmy brushed back her red hair. "The way the accelerator hit the floor, I'd say someone tampered with the throttle return spring on the carburetor. And to make sure we wouldn't stop, he or *they* made sure the brakes would fail."

"Sounds elaborate."

"I could do it to any car in under a minute."

"Max!" Frank shouted with a slap on his knee. "He came back covered with dirt and sweat, as though he'd been working hard and fast on something."

Emmy shook her head. "Forget it, Frank. He probably got that way from looking for the clutch plate. Besides, Max is a walking vanilla wafer. He's all peace, love, and harmony. He still thinks it's the 1960s. He's a harmless old hippie."

"If that's true, then why didn't the car go out of control before we got to Paradise Salvage?" he asked.

Emmy leaned against the cab and crossed her legs. "Good point. It would take only a couple of minutes to snip the throttle return spring, punch a hole in the brake line, and cut the emergency brake cable with bolt cutters."

"And Max had more than enough time," Frank added.

"You're right," Emmy conceded.

They rode in silence the remainder of the way to Royce's Garage.

"This place could use a real cleaning up," Frank said as he pushed open the office door and kicked at a pile of soiled red rags.

"Hey! Watch how you treat my place," Emmy protested.

"Your place? You mean the city's."

"I mean *mine*, as in I own this garage."

"Royce's Garage really does belong to you?"

"Why is that so hard for you to believe,

Frank?" Emmy stood with her hands on her hips, challenging him.

"Who was Royce?" Frank's mind was racing.

"He was my father," Emmy said before she could stop herself. Then she said quickly, "I've got to clean up. Bathroom's over there." She unlocked the inner office and slammed the door shut. Frank heard the lock click on the other side.

The hot water and soap lather stung the little cuts left on his face by the sharp concrete slivers, but it felt good to wipe away the grime of the accident.

Pieces were beginning to fall into place, but Frank wasn't sure what the final picture would be. Emmy had personal reasons for wanting to solve this case, and Frank just hoped her reasons didn't clash with his search for Chet.

Something in the cracked mirror caught his eye. At first he thought some giant bug with two large wings was floating behind him. He turned and stared at two photographs pinned to the wall across the bathroom.

He patted his face dry as he neared the photos and stared.

One of the photos was of the twisted remains of an old 1950s classic. Enough of it remained so that Frank could identify it as a Buick. Its hood was crumpled, the roof caved in, the massive chrome grille and bumper crumpled like cardboard, and the front fenders, their round chrome "portholes," smashed. The car had been rolled several times in a terrible accident.

The other photo was older and showed the Buick in better days, its bulky chrome and black and pink paint shining like mirrors.

Three people were gathered around the car, smiling like old friends. A teenage Emmy, her long red hair pulled back into a ponytail, sat on the massive hood. A stranger stood next to her—Royce Sauter? The third person in the photo sent chills up and down Frank's spine.

Butch Smith!

A thought shot through Frank's mind like a poisoned dart. Perhaps the reason why Cronkite's Auto Theft Division hadn't been able to break the chop shop ring was because the car thieves knew every move the police made—as they made them.

Frank snatched up the older photo, put it into his shirt pocket, and headed quietly out the front door.

Perhaps Emerson Sauter was working for her old friend, Butch Smith!

Chapter

9

JOE HARDY RESTRAINED the mounting anger that was growing within him. He squeezed the remote control garage door opener a block from Smith's chop shop—the plastic box cracked between his fingers.

Snake's bump-and-rob stunt had not only frightened an old woman, it may have ended Frank and Joe's chances of finding Chet. The victim had gotten a long, good, clean look at Joe. She'd be able to give the police an accurate description.

Cronkite wouldn't hesitate to throw Joe in the darkest, deepest pit of the Southport jail.

Joe's timing was perfect. The garage door was wide open as he jerked the steering wheel and guided the stolen Caddy into the warehouse opening.

Smith raised his hand in a friendly gesture. His smile and wave quickly gave way to an expression of stunned horror as Joe aimed the car for him and Snake. They scurried aside like frightened rabbits.

Joe stomped on the brakes. He pressed the remote control and the garage door started down.

Joe bolted from the car and headed for Snake. He stopped as Smith stepped in front of him.

"You know what your 'partner in slime' did?" Joe protested. "He assaults an old woman, steals a second car, and leaves me there holding the bag."

"Big deal." Smith shrugged.

Joe glared at Smith.

"You've got to relax, Joe, and go with the flow." Smith reached into his back pocket and pulled out a folded wad of bills two inches thick. "This ought to cool you off for a while." He flipped through the bills, all hundreds, and didn't stop until he had counted off fifteen. He handed the money to Joe.

Joe hesitated, then grabbed the bills, and stuffed them into his pocket.

"Not bad money for a couple hours' work." Smith chuckled. "Tell your brother that the Davises are now full-fledged members of the Smith Auto Redistribution Club."

"Thanks," Joe said with a sneer.

Smith started for the cars. "These two babies will keep Snake and me busy for a while." He picked up a cutting torch and fired it to life. He adjusted the blue-and-orange flame until it was a nearly invisible pencil-thin thread of destruction. "Well? What are you waiting for?"

Now that Frank and Joe were in, Joe decided to go one step further. He knew he was taking a risk, but he couldn't help the nagging feeling that time was running out for Chet.

"When do we see the other end of the operation?"

"What?" Smith asked above the roar of the torch.

"Frank and I want in on the deliveries," Joe shouted.

Smith shut off the torch and the warehouse became deadly silent. He walked slowly toward Joe, his eyes as cold as the silence.

"All in due time," Smith said. "You two play your cards right and you'll be vice presidents of my Bayport operations. Until then, lay low. And don't get greedy."

Smith relit the torch inches from Joe, the flame popping into a deadly flash. Joe remained still. Smith was testing his nerves, and Joe wasn't about to let the older man see him flinch.

Smith laughed and returned to the two cars.

Joe knew he had to find Frank and tell him they were in the gang. He didn't look forward to telling his older brother about the bump-and-rob.

Joe hopped in the van and pulled away from the curb.

"You boys certainly have some high-tech stuff back here," came a voice from the rear of the van.

Joe twisted around just enough to keep one eye on the street and peer back into the van with the other.

Cronkite waddled to the front and sat in the passenger seat.

"What are you doing here?" Joe asked nervously. He sensed that Cronkite knew about the bump-and-rob. "I can explain about the sports car," Joe quickly added.

"I'll just bet you can," Cronkite said as he propped one foot on the van's clean dash. "But save it. There's something I want to tell you *and* your brother."

"Where is Frank?"

"I had a patrol car pick him up as he was leaving Royce's. He's waiting for us at Don's Daylight Donuts. Turn here." Cronkite pointed.

Minutes later Frank and Joe sat in a dingy booth at Don's Daylight Donuts. The bakery was old, and the walls were dark with dirt and the grime of years of greasy smoke. Cronkite sat across from the Hardys, stuffing a jelly doughnut into his mouth.

"Give me one, just one good reason why I shouldn't yank you two off this case, and I mean *now,*" Cronkite mumbled through the doughnut.

"How about—" Joe began.

"How about keeping your mouth shut!" Cronkite fired back. "You can't give me *any* reason to keep you yahoos in Southport any longer. While Frank was running *my* car off a bridge and into a dry riverbed, Joe was playing bump-and-rob with Snake. They nearly killed an old woman in the process."

Frank and Joe exchanged glances. They had a lot to tell each other.

"What are you two? A wrecking crew?" Cronkite leaned back in his chair. "You going to eat that doughnut?" he asked Frank.

"We didn't come here to stuff our faces, Detective," Frank replied.

Cronkite snatched the doughnut and bit into it. "You're just lucky that old woman wasn't wearing her glasses or she would have given our police artist a better description of you. As it is, we're all out looking for a short, fat teenager with freckles and his partner, a skinny long-haired kid with large black eyes. I ought to take you both in.''

"You won't do that," Joe said, his arms crossed.

"Oh, yeah? And why not, wiseguy?"

"Well, for one thing, you'll have a hard time explaining to your captain why you allowed two 'kids' to go undercover on a dangerous chop shop operation," Frank remarked.

Cronkite began coughing as he choked on his mouthful.

"And for another," Joe added, "Frank and I are one step away from discovering who's fencing Smith's chopped parts."

Cronkite cleared his throat. His eyes had watered, and his voice cracked. "How close?"

"We'll make you a deal," Frank spoke up. "You stop interfering and we'll deliver Smith *and* his silent partner in forty-eight hours."

Cronkite stared at Frank. "Forty-eight hours?"

"Just two days," Joe said.

"Don't get smart, wiseguy," Cronkite shot back. "Okay," he conceded. "But if you two don't have something by late Thursday, I'm yanking you off the case."

"You sure you haven't promised something we can't deliver?" Joe asked Frank as they drove back to their motel.

"We need time to find Chet," Frank answered. "Is Smith happy with our talents?"

"Tickled pink. In fact"—Joe reached into his front pocket—"he's given us some cash."

Frank whistled as he counted off the bills. "We should have given this to Cronkite to mark as evidence."

"I know. But I was so intent on convincing Cronkite to keep us on, I forgot about it. We can give it to him later."

The digital car phone chirped, and Frank snatched it up.

"Hello."

"Frank? Joe? This is Uncle Ed." The tremble in the man's voice told Frank that Uncle Ed was in a near panic.

"What is it, Uncle Ed?"

"I got . . . another phone call. He—the kidnapper—is going to kill Chet if I don't do as he says."

"Where are you?"

"At my office."

"Stay there. We're on our way."

Ten minutes later the van pulled into the parking lot of AutoHaus Emporium. Frank and Joe found Uncle Ed pacing in circles on the office carpet.

"He called about fifteen minutes ago," Uncle Ed explained. "He sounded very mean. I know he's going to hurt Chet."

"Did you write down his instructions?" Joe asked.

"Write it down?" Uncle Ed seemed confused.

"Yes," Frank said. "Did you write down what the kidnapper wanted."

"No."

Frank and Joe shook their heads.

"I recorded it," Uncle Ed added.

"Recorded it?" Frank asked.

"Yes. My answering machine automatically records all my phone conversations. I make so many deals for specialty cars over the phone that I need a record of the transactions. Do you want to hear the conversation?"

Frank nodded and smiled. He liked Uncle Ed, even if the older man was a bit odd.

Uncle Ed punched the REWIND and then the PLAY button on his answering machine.

The kidnapper's voice was rough, deep, and vicious. Frank and Joe looked at each other and shrugged. They didn't recognize the voice.

The kidnapper's terms were simple. Uncle Ed was to hand over one hundred thousand dollars.

Uncle Ed demanded to talk to Chet. For the first time in four days, Frank and Joe heard the voice of their old friend.

What they heard sent chills up and down their spines.

"H-hello," Chet said weakly.

"Chet? Chet, are you okay?" Uncle Ed all but shouted on the tape.

"Uncle Ed?" They could hear Chet smacking his lips and tongue, a sign that he was thirsty.

Uncle Ed's voice was hysterical. "I'll get you out of this, son, just don't do anything foolish."

"Uncle Ed?" Chet gasped.

"Yes, son," Uncle Ed replied softly. "How are you?"

"I'm—okay. Don't listen to this creep."

"Give me that." They heard the kidnapper growl. "Stupid kid."

The next sounds were a fleshy smack and a deep moan from Chet. The kidnapper had hit Chet.

"One hundred thousand dollars, Brooke," the kidnapper growled.

"W-where? When?"

"Just get it! Be ready to go when I call again tomorrow—three P.M. *If* you want to see your nephew alive again."

The phone clicked dead. A horrified gasp from Uncle Ed and the hissing static from the phone line were the last sounds on the tape.

The recorder shut itself off with a loud click.

Frank had promised Cronkite to deliver the fence in forty-eight hours. He was hoping to buy time to find Chet. Time, however, was not a friendly ally to the Hardys. Uncle Ed had to have one hundred thousand dollars by the next day.

Or Chet Morton would end up dead.

Chapter

10

FRANK TAPPED the cassette tape in his hand. He had asked to keep it so he could listen again. Something about the conversation bothered him. But what?

For the last half hour, Frank had sat in the motel room replaying the tape on his portable pocket cassette player. He had to control his anger as he listened over and over to the kidnapper hitting Chet.

He had to ignore that and concentrate. He had to sift through the voices and words and noise to filter out any clues.

Nothing.

He stabbed at the OFF button and threw the tape player on his bed next to the photo he had swiped from Royce's. Another unsolved mystery.

The door was unlocked and Joe entered, a large brown paper bag in one hand.

"Dinner," he announced.

"I'm not hungry." Frank stared out the window.

"Heard nothing new on the tape?"

Frank's silence answered Joe's question.

Joe placed the bag on Frank's bed and sat across on his own. He opened up the bag and pulled out a hamburger, fries, and a soft drink. Frank might be able to go without food, but Joe couldn't.

Joe picked up the photo lying next to the tape player—the photo of Emmy, an older man next to her, and Smith.

"You really think Emmy's working both sides of the law?" Joe asked between bites of the burger.

Frank sighed. "I don't know. She has opportunity."

"What about motive?"

"Oldest motive in the world."

"Greed," Joe said in answer to his own question.

"Right. What I haven't been able to figure out is her connection with Smith. If they're such old friends, why hasn't she been able to join his gang, work undercover in his operation instead of trying to run her own shop?"

Joe shrugged. He looked at Frank. "What else is bothering you?"

"That man next to Emmy. I'm positive he's her father."

"You think he's mixed up in this somehow?"

"No."

"Why not?"

"Because he's dead."

"Emmy tell you that?" Joe asked.

"No. While you were getting dinner, I called vital records at city hall. Royce Sauter died seven months ago. The clerk wouldn't say how, but I can guess. There was another picture next to this one, except the car looked like it had been in a terrible accident."

"So?"

"Emmy's hiding something. She avoids talking directly about her father or the garage or anything to do with her past."

"Any idea who sabotaged Cronkite's car?"

"Max. He had plenty of time, and he looked too dirty to have been looking for a clutch plate. But Emmy doesn't think so."

"Why not?"

"She thinks he's too flaky," Frank replied.

"Why not Cronkite?"

"Cronkite?"

Joe put his drink down. "It's just a hunch, but Cronkite always seems to be right there when something's happening. Why would he lend Emmy his car?"

The beeper chirped. Frank grabbed the black box and shut it off. "I'll call this time," he said as he picked up the phone.

Joe gulped down his cold soft drink. He felt guilty eating and drinking while Chet was lying hurt someplace, probably hungry and thirsty.

He suddenly wasn't hungry any longer. He threw what remained of his burger and fries into the bag, wadded it up, and tossed the whole thing into the trash.

"That was Smith. He wants to meet us at a place downtown called Skyway Parking Garage," Frank said after hanging up the phone. He grabbed the tape and the photo and stuffed them both into his shirt pocket.

"Did he say why?" Joe asked.

"No. But this may be our chance to see the delivery end of the operation."

"Looks abandoned," Frank said as he leaned forward and strained his neck to look up the ten stories of the garage. Skyway Parking was only a few blocks from Don's Daylight Donuts, near the center of Southport.

"What better place than a large, empty parking garage to hide stolen parts," Joe said.

"Or a kidnap victim." Frank leaned back in

his seat. "Smith wants to meet us at the top level."

Joe eased the van around a wooden barricade, ignoring the NO TRESPASSING signs, and wound the van up the parking garage.

"What's really beginning to bother me," Frank said, "is if Emmy *is* involved with Smith, if she is a bad cop, why would her car have been sabotaged this morning?"

It was a good question for which Joe had no answer.

"Who would target Emmy, and why?" Frank was talking more to himself than Joe.

"Perhaps Emmy wasn't the one they were after," Joe said.

"What?"

The thought that he was the intended target had crossed Frank's mind earlier, but hearing it from Joe, out loud for the first time, stunned him. Except for Uncle Ed, Emmy, and Cronkite, he was unknown in Southport. The only person who would want Frank out of the way would be the leader of the chop shop ring. And as far as Frank was concerned, he had a trio of suspects: Smith, Max, and Emmy.

"Now what?" Joe asked as he brought the van to a halt on the top level of the parking garage. He hopped out and scouted the area.

Frank remained seated and stared at the

dash, letting his vision blur. Why not two bad cops? Emmy *and* Cronkite? he thought.

"Hey," Joe said with a light tap on Frank's shoulder.

Frank jumped as if startled from a deep sleep.

"What's wrong?" Joe asked.

Frank stepped from the van. He jogged to the edge of the parking lot and leaned over the railing.

"Did you see anyone following us?" he asked, rejoining Joe.

"No," Joe replied. "What's up?"

"I don't think we can trust anyone in the Southport Police Department."

"Why not?"

Before Frank could answer, the quiet early evening stillness was shattered by a thunderous rumble. A half second later a black TransAm burst from the access ramp. Like some great hungry beast seeking its prey, it zeroed in on the Hardys.

Frank and Joe dove in opposite directions, the TransAm missing them by inches.

By the time they had regained their footing, the car had spun 180 degrees and was pointed at them once again.

Two men jumped from the car. They were the same height and wore identical gray suits. Dark sunglasses hid their eyes. They were mirror images of each other, except for their hair—and the guns they aimed at Frank and Joe.

The black-haired man, the driver, held a .45 while his red-haired partner stood on the passenger side with a sawed-off semiautomatic shotgun.

"Frank and Joe Hardy!" Blackie yelled out across the parking lot. "Got any last requests?"

"Yeah," shouted Red. "You can start your prayers now."

Frank and Joe looked at each other. They were easy targets. The van sat thirty yards away. It might as well have been a mile. No matter how fast they ran, they wouldn't be able to outrun the wide spread of the sawed-off shotgun blast.

"Goodbye," Blackie shouted as though to old friends.

The calm twilight erupted with a thunderous roar of death from the .45 and the shotgun.

Chapter

11

FRANK FELL TO THE PAVEMENT and rolled away, shotgun pellets striking the concrete inches from him. He was on his feet and zigzagging toward the van, Joe at his shoulder.

A bullet clipped the heel of Frank's shoe and he sprawled on the ground, smacking into the concrete. Dazed, he tried to lift himself.

Blackie smiled, clutched the .45 with both hands, leaned on the open driver's door, and slowly took careful aim at Frank.

"Police! Drop it!" a high-pitched voice shouted. Joe recognized Emmy's voice above the roar of the gunfire. A split second later a third gun erupted.

Blackie fell back behind the protection of the car door.

A slug from Emmy's gun slammed into

Red's left leg, twisting the gunman around in a violent spasm.

Joe pulled Frank up and both bolted toward the van.

Blackie no longer concentrated his fire at the Hardys but somewhere behind them.

Joe glanced over his shoulder. Emmy stood in the opening of the garage's stairwell, her police .38 smoking and blazing. She ducked back into the doorway as several slugs from the .45 chipped at the concrete frame around her.

Having recovered, Red turned his shotgun on the fleeing Hardys while Blackie kept Emmy pinned back inside the stairwell.

Frank and Joe reached the van as a shotgun blast peppered the side of the van, chipping the black paint on the van's armored siding.

Joe jumped into the driver's seat, Frank into the passenger's.

"Let's go!" Frank yelled as he slammed his door shut.

Joe threw the transmission into reverse and stomped on the accelerator. The tires screamed, and the van shot backward.

The van echoed with the *ping, ping, ping* from another shotgun blast.

"What are you doing?" Frank yelled.

"We've got to get Emmy! Open up the side door!"

Emmy! Frank had had the feeling they were being tailed. He shook his head sadly. Emmy had set them up.

Frank twisted in his seat and flung the panel door open. Joe slammed on the brakes and the van squealed to a halt in front of the stairwell opening.

Emmy vaulted into the van. She slammed the panel door shut as Joe pushed the shift lever into drive and rocketed away from the stairwell.

The van hit the access ramp with such speed that it flew into the air, then bounced with such force that its shocks and springs groaned against the sudden full impact of the van's weight.

"What are you doing here?" Frank shouted at Emmy.

"I—" Emmy began.

"Never mind," Joe interrupted. "We've got company."

Frank looked in his side mirror. The TransAm was bearing down on them. Joe was doing a good job jockeying the van around the hairpin turns as they descended out of the parking lot, but the lighter, smaller car was closing in.

Red stuck the shotgun out his window and fired.

Joe swerved the van to the left and the

pellets scraped down Frank's side, shattering Frank's mirror.

The TransAm slammed into the rear of the van. Joe twisted the steering wheel left and right to keep the van from smashing into a concrete wall.

"Got any ammo?" Emmy yelled. "I'm out."

"No," Frank replied. "I've got something better."

Frank hopped to the back of the van and flipped open the tool box. He pulled out a small but heavy crowbar.

The van jolted as the TransAm rammed into it again.

Frank and Emmy grabbed each other to keep from falling over.

For one brief moment, Frank saw genuine fear and panic in Emmy's eyes and face. Could this be the face that had betrayed them?

"When I give the signal," Frank shouted, "open the back door."

"But—"

"Just do it!" Frank steadied himself and cocked back his arm. *Now!*

Emmy threw open the door.

With all the strength he could muster, Frank flung the crowbar in a deadly spinning arc toward the TransAm's windshield.

A look of surprise and horror crossed the

two gunmen's faces. The crowbar smashed into the windshield, turning the shatterproof glass into a useless white mass of hairline cracks that covered the entire windshield.

Blackie lost control of the car and slammed into the side of a concrete wall. The car's hood crumpled and exploded open. One corner of the hood caught the air cleaner, ripping it from atop the carburetor. The fuel line leading to the carburetor broke loose, and gasoline sprayed the top of the hot engine. A second later flames erupted and grew larger, fed by the spewing gas from the fuel line.

The car scraped against a concrete wall. The entire engine compartment was in flames, and angry black smoke surrounded the TransAm.

Satisfied that the gunmen were out of commission, Frank closed the rear door.

Joe crashed the van through the wooden barricades and NO TRESPASSING signs and turned the van out onto the street. The van tilted on two wheels, then fell back hard on all four.

"Head for Royce's," Emmy yelled as she threw herself onto the small bench just behind Joe.

Frank eased his way forward and into his seat and turned to face her.

"Want to tell me what you were doing at the

parking garage?" Frank's voice was steady, accusing.

"Saving your lives," Emmy replied with a smile.

"Were you?" Frank's eyes were hard, piercing.

Emmy's smile dropped. "Yes. I was."

Frank pulled the photo from his pocket. "Want to explain this?"

Emmy looked confused, then outraged. She snatched the photo from Frank.

"That's mine." Her voice was cold.

"The man next to you is your father, isn't he?" Emmy remained silent. "What's your connection with Smith?"

Emmy's reply was venomous. "That's *my* business, Frank."

"Now I'm making it ours," Frank replied, nodding toward Joe. "We've got a friend whose life is on the line. No one knew Joe and I were going to the garage except Smith. Then you show up. You've been tailing us. Why?"

Emmy's eyes narrowed as the full understanding of Frank's implication sank in.

"The photo proves you've known Smith for years. When did you transfer to the Southport Police Department, Emmy? Wasn't it just a few weeks after your father's accident?" Frank was playing a hunch. He had to find out what Emmy knew about Smith.

Emmy's creamy complexion turned a deep red. She was shaking with anger.

"I'll say this only once, Frank Hardy." Emmy took a deep breath and let it hiss out slowly. Her icy green eyes flickered and her bottom lip quavered. "I'm a cop. A *good* cop. And because I'm a good cop, I tailed you two hoping to get a lead on Smith's fence. Instead I end up pulling you two out of a death trap."

"And Smith?"

"Smith is a creep I knew a long time ago. I was the one who told Cronkite about him and his little chop shop business."

"You knew about the chop shop before you transferred from New York to Southport?"

"Not exactly, but I had a hunch. Smith was convicted of operating a chop shop five years ago. He wasn't out of prison a month when this latest one opened up. No one in Southport knew I was a cop. Cronkite thought it the perfect cover. I take over my father's auto repair and body shop and try to get inside Smith's gang."

"Why didn't it work?" Joe asked.

Emmy wouldn't relax. Months of frustration poured from her. "I don't know. Even though we've known each other for years, Smith won't have anything to do with me, except offering to buy my garage last week."

"You still think Max had nothing to do with

sabotaging your car this morning?'' Frank was beginning to change his mind about Emmy.

"I'm not sure about anything or any*body*." Emmy stared hard at Frank.

"How did you know our last name is Hardy? Cronkite told you it was Davis."

Emmy swallowed. "I had my suspicions about you two after the accident at the bridge. Cronkite told me your last name. Unlike you, Frank, Cronkite trusts me."

Frank felt that Emmy was still hiding something.

Emmy choked back a sob.

"How did the accident happen?" Frank asked softly.

"It wasn't an accident," Emmy replied. "My father was murdered!"

Chapter

12

FRANK FELT about two inches tall. He had been ready to accuse Emmy of working with Smith. Instead, she had risked her own life to save him and Joe.

Now she sat trembling before him, trying to control her pain as she recalled the murder of her father, Royce Sauter.

"My father was murdered," Emmy repeated slowly. "A school bus driver said that he saw my father's car approaching the bus stop at high speed. Kids were unloading, crossing the road to the other side. The driver said my father had obviously lost control of the car.

"My father had only two choices—the kids or an unfinished off ramp. He swerved off the road, away from the bus and the kids, hit the off ramp, flipped, and rolled one hundred fifty feet. He was dead at the scene."

"I'm sorry," Frank said. He cleared his throat. "What happened?"

"The papers said it was a heart attack." Emmy gulped in air and held her breath for a few moments. Frank could tell she was fighting back tears. "I found out after I transferred to Southport that the reason my father's car lost control was because it had been sabotaged."

"The same guy who sabotaged Cronkite's car this morning?" Frank asked.

"Maybe," Emmy said.

"Why did the police keep the murder a secret?" Frank asked.

"Cronkite wanted it that way. My father had been letting him use his shop as a front. Someone must have found out and killed him. I inherited the garage and went undercover."

Frank reached over and gripped Emmy's trembling shoulder. "I'm sorry."

They pulled up to Royce's Garage. The old cinder-block building took on a new and special meaning for Frank. He could imagine the many happy hours Emmy and her father had spent in the garage, all brought to a halt by his murder.

Once they had found Chet, Frank vowed, he would help Emmy find the man who had killed her father.

As the trio approached the office door, Cronkite stepped out, his temples pulsing rapidly from anger and the gum he was smacking.

"Well, if it isn't the Bayport wrecking crew." Cronkite's smile was plastic, mocking.

Emmy remained silent, pushed past Cronkite, and entered the inner office, slamming the door shut.

Frank was about to follow when Cronkite cut him off.

"You two yahoos want to explain yourselves this time?"

Frank and Joe ignored the question.

Cronkite pulled on his mustache. "You know what I just heard on my car radio? Some citizens reported a gun battle at the Skyway Parking Garage. They also saw a black van leaving the scene. By the time my officers arrived, all they found was a burning TransAm. No driver. No bodies. You two wouldn't happen to know anything about that, would you?"

"We got a call from Smith," Joe said. "He wanted to meet us there."

"Why?" Cronkite asked.

"We never found out," Joe said. "Two gunmen showed up and tried to kill us."

Cronkite seemed unconcerned. "Maybe you can ask him tomorrow morning," he said.

"What do you mean?" Frank asked.

"We're busting Smith's place, at dawn, just like the cavalry."

"You can't do that," Joe protested.

Cronkite snorted. "Oh, yeah? And why not?"

"He's our only link to Chet," Frank replied.

"That's not your problem any longer. You two are out as of this minute."

"I thought we had forty-eight hours," Frank said.

"Forget it. The captain's real anxious to close this case."

"What about Max? Emmy thinks Smith may be using the salvage yard hotline to move the parts." Frank had the uneasy feeling that his hunch about Cronkite was right.

"Max? That cornflake?" Cronkite laughed.

"You've got to give us a little more time," Joe said sternly.

"The only thing I got to do," Cronkite replied, his bulldog face squeezed into a tight frown, his finger thumping Joe on the chest, "is make sure you two cowboys don't get in my way."

"Let's get out of here, Joe," Frank said before Joe could say anything. "It's obvious that Detective Cronkite is right. We'll just be in the way."

Joe knew his brother well enough to realize that Frank was putting on an act. He didn't know what Frank was scheming, but he trusted Frank and would go along with him. He followed his brother to the van.

"Uh, Frank," Cronkite said from the doorway of the office. Frank turned. "I would think such a smart 'detective' as you would know better than to withhold evidence."

"What are you talking about?"

"I stopped by Brooke's place before I came here. That man can't keep a secret." He held out his hand. "I'll take the tape, if you don't mind."

"It's at the motel," Frank lied.

Cronkite turned the answer over in his head for a moment, then sneered, "Just make sure it gets into the proper hands."

Frank and Joe hopped into the van. The detective gave a mocking, insincere wave as they pulled away from Royce's Garage.

"So, what's brewing?" Joe asked after they had gone several blocks.

Frank fingered the tape. Something about the background noise bothered him, but that would have to wait.

"Head for the motel," he replied. "We'll get a few hours' rest and then start the raiding party a little bit earlier than planned."

"You read my mind." Joe smiled as he gassed the van.

*   *   *

Frank and Joe stood outside the dark and empty chop shop dressed in the black pullovers and pants they kept in the van for nighttime surveillance. They canvassed the outside of the building, trying to find an easy way in. The building was large, and the early-morning full moon threw deep shadows down the side of the building. They stopped in the back alley.

Joe glanced at his watch. "This place is going to be crawling with cops in about an hour."

"When they get here," Frank began, wrapping a handkerchief around his right fist, "they're going to have to file a breaking and entering report."

Without hesitation, he smashed his hand through one of the blackened windows. Glass shards shattered on the concrete floor inside the warehouse.

Joe looked up and down the alley. "All clear."

Frank reached through the broken pane, carefully avoiding the razor-sharp edges, unlocked the window, and threw it open.

He and Joe climbed inside and stood in the large, dark, open warehouse. Joe flipped on his penlight. The metal skeleton of Uncle Ed's Caddy sat on blocks, parts lying around it, some in boxes, some in the open. The old woman's sports car was nowhere to be seen.

They sprinted across the warehouse to Smith's office.

Frank turned the doorknob. Locked. He had expected as much. He stepped back and kicked the door open.

Joe stepped inside, shut the door, and flipped on the light. Except for a metal desk, a chair, and a wastepaper basket, the office was empty.

No Chet.

Joe wasn't really expecting to find his friend in the office, but he was still disappointed.

"Maybe there's something in the desk," Frank said, reading the frustration in Joe's face. The desk was nearly as empty as the office. A phone, several bills, and an auto parts catalog were on the desktop; the drawers were empty. Frank sat down at the desk. He was puzzled by a large rectangular area of dust on the desk.

Upset by the lack of clues and the stone wall they seemed to have run up against, Joe grabbed the thick catalog and flung it across the office.

"I don't know what you expected to find," Frank said, thumbing through the stack of bills on the desk as he continued to eye the dusty spot. "It's not as though Smith would keep a record of stolen parts lying around."

"You're right." Joe kicked the wastebasket. "But you'd think there'd be *something*.

They're moving three, four cars a week here. And we're not talking station wagons and sedans, but expensive, classy cars. I don't care what Cronkite says, Smith has someone fencing the parts for him. Even crooks keep tabs to make sure their thieving friends don't steal from them."

Frank wasn't listening. He was staring at the large dusty spot. Something about the shape looked familiar. He closed his eyes and tried to remember where he had seen that shape before.

Frank's face lit up in a smile.

"What is it?" Joe asked.

"Remember last spring when Aunt Gertrude made us clean *everything* in our rooms?"

"What about it?"

Frank ignored the impatience in Joe's voice and traced the outline of the rectangle. "You know how clean I keep my desk, especially the area around my computer. After Aunt Gertrude insisted I take everything off my desk, I found that dust had gathered under my computer."

"So what?" Joe said.

"It looked just like this," Frank replied, continuing to trace the dusty rectangle.

"Then there is a record!" Joe was suddenly excited. "But where's the computer?"

"Someone must have tipped Smith about the raid, and he took the computer with him."

"He could have just burned the floppy discs," Joe said.

"Smith doesn't seem to be the type who would bother with floppy discs. My guess is that he had a hard drive."

"He still could have erased the hard drive's memory."

"If you had thousands of dollars of inventory on a hard drive, would you dump it all?" Frank didn't wait for Joe to answer. "It's easier to carry the computer out and start all over someplace else."

"Didn't you say that Paradise Salvage used a computer to track down car parts?" Joe asked.

Frank picked up the phone bill and flipped it open. He smiled again. The phone bill recorded hundreds of dollars' worth of computer modem charges from Smith's garage to a rural number outside of Southport. Frank picked up the phone and dialed the number.

The other end rang several times.

"Come on, come on," Frank grumbled.

"Hello," a man's sleepy voice finally said.

Then the garage was filled with a grating noise. The uproar drowned out the man's voice. Frank slammed the phone into its cradle.

"The garage door." Joe's whisper was barely audible above the clamor. He turned off the light.

He cracked the door just enough so he and Frank could peer across the warehouse floor.

A thin man stood silhouetted against the large opening, the dull yellow of a lone streetlight casting the man's shadow the entire length of the warehouse.

The garage door reached the top and stopped. The renewed silence was deadly.

The thin man lifted what appeared to be a five-gallon can. He poured liquid from it on the wooden crates and stacks of tires. He tossed the rest on the fifty-gallon drums of toxic solvent and pressurized oxygen-acetylene tanks.

Once the can was emptied, he tossed it toward the back of the warehouse. The can bounced and spun and slid until it hit the office door with a thud.

Vapors from the can burned Joe's eyes and throat.

The man lit a match, the flame's yellowish glow illuminating the pinched features of Snake, his face twisted in a triumphant smile.

Snake tossed the match to the floor. An eerie *whoosh!* filled the garage, and Snake disappeared behind a wall of angry thick flames.

In two seconds the flames fanned out through the warehouse, lapping up the gasoline in a feverish gorge, engulfing the wooden crates, tires, fifty-gallon drums, and welding tanks.

The crunching of the flames was joined by a loud grating as the garage door began its descent—trapping Frank and Joe inside a giant, monstrous furnace!

Chapter

13

FRANK AND JOE bolted toward the closing garage door. The inferno cut them off from the doorway and the windows around the garage. Flames and heat chased them back to the office.

Joe flipped on his penlight. "No windows here!" he said, coughing.

Smoke was filling the small office space. The Hardys fell to the floor, where the air was fresher.

The white paint on the plywood walls turned brown, then cracked and bubbled and smoked. The plywood itself began to pop as it reached its ignition point, finally bursting into flames.

"The ceiling!" Frank shouted above the infernal roar.

Joe followed Frank's finger. The ceiling was nothing more than suspended cork tiles.

"Maybe we can climb through to the beams and work our way behind the flames to one of the windows," Frank explained.

They jumped to their feet. Frank leapt on top of the desk and punched a ceiling tile with both fists. It crumbled to the floor, dusting Joe.

Frank sprung up, grabbed a steel beam, and hoisted himself free of the office. He moved aside as Joe jumped up and grabbed a beam.

Joe had no sooner pulled himself through the opening when the office walls collapsed inward, tearing down the ceiling as well.

Like skilled aerialists, Frank and Joe made their way, hand over hand, across the garage to the window Frank had broken minutes before.

"It's blocked!" Frank shouted. "We've got to go back."

"Where? The whole place is on fire!"

Joe was right. The fire was raging out of control. Every square inch of the floor and walls was covered with burning oil and solvent and tires. Even the steel beams were getting hot, slowly burning their hands.

"There!" Frank shouted, pointing.

Ten feet ahead of them, in the garage's ceiling, was a trap door that led to the roof.

"I see it!" Joe shouted, choking from the fumes.

Cautiously, they made their way toward the trap door. They ignored the pain of the hot steel beams, the toxic smoke, and the fire that snapped at them from below.

Frank reached the small square door. He boosted himself on top of the beam and pushed up. It was locked. "Hold me!" he yelled.

Joe boosted himself up, too, and held on to the back of Frank's shirt.

Frank forced out all thoughts of the garage and the fire and the pain. The words of his karate instructor floated to the front of his mind.

Think through the object. Imagine your fist already on the other side.

With a terrifying scream and lightning quickness, Frank's jackhammer fist shattered the plywood door; the pieces fell and were instantly consumed by the flames.

He pulled himself through and then helped Joe out.

They rolled away from the opening, coughing out the smoke and poison fumes and sucking in large quantities of fresh air.

The tar on the roof began to melt. They hopped up and ran to the edge. The ground was twenty feet below them and solid concrete.

The roof heaved as an explosion rocked the building.

"The welding tanks!" Frank shouted. "They're like bombs."

They ran to the alley side of the garage. The drop was still twenty feet, but across the narrow alley was a Dumpster full of trash from a fast-food joint.

"It's our only chance," Frank said.

They backed away from the edge and jumped toward the Dumpster.

The soft, decaying food broke the impact of their fall. Garbage flew into the air and covered Frank and Joe.

"*Yuck!* What a smell." Joe pulled rotting bread and lettuce from his hair.

The crackling of the fire was joined by the sirens of fire engines.

Frank and Joe ran to the end of the alley and into their van. In seconds, stinking of smoke and rotting food, they were headed away from the fire—slowly, so as not to arouse suspicion.

Joe pulled a green leafy substance from his shirt pocket. "All of that, and we still don't know where Chet is!"

"Think again," Frank replied, using the phone bill as a fan to cool himself.

Joe shook his head and smiled.

Frank grabbed the van's cellular phone and punched the number on the lighted digital buttons. He hit the intercom so Joe could hear.

It rang twice and the same sleepy voice said, "Hello. Paradise Salvage."

Frank hung up.

"Just a harmless old hippie," Joe spat out.

"Yeah." Frank combed his hair back with his fingers. "I had a feeling about Max yesterday, but Emmy and Cronkite had almost convinced me I was wrong." He held up the phone bill. "This doesn't prove Max's got Chet, but it does prove Max and Smith are connected."

Joe perked up. "Look who we have here."

A block ahead of the van, leaning against the old woman's sports car, in front of a lighted telephone booth, stood Snake.

Joe gunned the van and jumped the curb. He hit the brakes, and the van squealed to a stop inches from Snake and the telephone booth.

Snake, his small eyes wide with horror, tried to pull open the sports car's door but his hand kept slipping on the pull-up latch.

Frank and Joe hopped from the van.

"What are you doing up so early, you worm?" Joe asked.

"Hey, guys. What's happening?" Snake's nose wrinkled up as Frank and Joe stood closer. *"Pee-yew!"* Snake tried to turn his head.

Joe jerked him back around. "Never mind that. Did you just torch the chop shop?"

Snake's beady black eyes shot back and forth between Frank and Joe.

"Y-y-yes!" He tried to smile.

"Why?" Frank demanded.

Snake swallowed hard. "Butch said that the cops were going to bust the place at sunrise."

"How did he know that?" Frank asked.

"I—I—don't know, man. Butch just said he wanted to give the cops a warm reception, that's all."

"What are you doing with the old woman's car?" Joe asked.

"We didn't have time to chop it. Butch said we'll do it at our new place."

"What new place?" Frank growled. He was getting tired of playing twenty questions.

"He—he said that we'd have another place pretty soon."

"Did Smith take a computer with him when you two cleared-out?" Frank asked.

"Yeah."

"Where's this new place?" Joe asked.

"I don't know. He just said that we'd have a new place after that chick cop was dead."

Frank's eyes widened. "What chick cop?"

"That Sauter creep, the one who's been bugging him. She's an undercover cop."

"Who told you she was a cop?" Frank asked, his eyes narrow slits of anger.

"Butch did. He's got someone working on the inside for him." He turned to leave, only to be stopped by Frank.

"You're coming with us," Frank said.

Snake twisted to pull away from Frank. He

took a roundhouse swing at Frank's head, and as close as they were, he missed.

With one quick karate jab, Frank sent Snake to dreamland. Then he hoisted Snake on one shoulder and dumped him into the back of the van. He tied Snake's ankles and wrists together and then joined Joe in the front.

"We're going to need some support if we raid Paradise Salvage," Frank said, his mind scheming the best way to get into the salvage yard unseen by Max or Smith.

"Emmy?" Joe asked.

"Yes."

"What about Cronkite?" Joe steered the van onto Main Street.

"I don't trust him."

"If he's the fourth member of the gang, the police mole, why would he tell us about the bust? Wouldn't he just tell Smith and let Smith torch the place?"

"That's a good point," Frank said. "I'm interested in seeing Cronkite's reaction when we bring Snake in. If Smith and Cronkite are partners, Cronkite will be upset to see Snake in custody."

"And if Snake is able to slither out of jail, we might have proof that Cronkite is working on the inside," Joe added.

"First," Frank said, holding his nose, "let's

get rid of this smell and shower and change clothes.''

Joe wrinkled his nose in agreement, and minutes later they were at the motel. While Joe headed up to the second-floor room, Frank jumped in the back of the van to check Snake. He was still out cold, the ropes tight around his wrists and ankles.

Frank stepped from the van and stretched. The sun was cresting behind the motel. A good hot shower and clean clothes sounded great.

He headed up the stairs to the second floor and was nearly knocked over by a man in a gray suit limping past him.

"Excuse me," Frank apologized.

The man hurried on, not bothering to acknowledge Frank's presence, let alone his apology.

Frank shook his head and climbed the stairs. He was too tired and too concerned about Chet to worry about the rudeness of the red-haired man.

Red!

Frank twisted around. "Hey!" he shouted.

Red hobbled away as fast as he could. Frank began to chase after him when he suddenly realized that he hadn't seen Joe on the second-floor landing.

He was up the stairs in three leaps. Joe lay in a crumpled heap half in, half out of their room. Frank dashed down the corridor. As he neared, he heard Joe groan.

"Easy," Frank said as he helped Joe to his feet.

Joe swayed. "Thanks," he moaned. "What happened?"

"From the lump on your head, I'd say Red thumped you a good one."

"Red?"

"Yeah. I guess he heard me coming and decided he couldn't handle both of us."

The roar of an engine and the crunch of gravel shattered the silence of the motel court. Frank watched as a dark Camaro peeled away from the Hardys' van.

A queasy feeling rumbled through Frank's stomach. He darted down the stairs and straight to the rear of the van.

Frank took a deep breath, hesitated, and threw open the doors.

Snake was on his side, just as Frank had left him. The early-morning sun highlighted the rattlesnake tattoo and its Born to Die motto on Snake's thin, pale arm. He lay motionless, his wrists and ankles bound, just as Frank had left him—almost.

Wrapped deadly tight around Snake's throat was an extra coil of rope.

Chapter

14

FRANK SAT on the hard mattress of the jail cell staring at the graffiti-covered, whitewashed walls. It was close to nine A.M. when the homicide detectives had brought Frank and Joe in. Frank spent two grueling hours trying to convince a skeptical and nearly hysterical Cronkite, as well as a hardboiled homicide detective, that he and Joe had not torched Smith's chop shop or killed Snake.

Cronkite wasn't convinced.

Then it had been Joe's turn.

Frank stood, stretched, and shook his head. He faced a cell wall, leaned against it, and began stretching his legs. They had to escape. They had to find Chet.

The clanking of the cell door startled Frank.

Joe stood at the bars, a fuming Cronkite on the other side. Frank joined them.

"I'd hate to be in your shoes right now," Cronkite said with a laugh. "The district attorney says this will be the easiest case he's had in years."

"All we tried to do," Frank began, "is find our friend. He's still in danger, and we think we know where he is."

"You beat everything, you know that? You're in jail on suspicion of arson and murder, and you're still trying to run the show. You think phone bills and a missing computer are proof? Smith's front was that he ran a repair shop. Of course he's going to call that nincompoop to ask about parts." Cronkite's voice cracked as he threw his hands up in disbelief.

"Just check it out," Frank said.

"Forget it.' Cronkite glanced at his watch. "When homicide is done with your van, I want you two and that armor-plated tank out of Southport." Cronkite stormed out through a steel door that separated the squad room from the holding cell.

Joe sat on the bunk and stared at his brother. Frank remained standing, leaning against the bars. They compared notes from their separate interrogations. They had told the same story, but Cronkite still blamed the Hardys for blowing the chop shop investigation.

"One good note," Frank said.

"What's that?" Joe grunted.

"We're not charged with arson or murder."

"How do you know that?"

"Would Cronkite be releasing us and the van if he really believed we were guilty of murder."

"No," Joe agreed.

"I rest my case."

"Well, you two are living proof that good looks and brains don't necessarily go together."

Frank and Joe spun around. Emmy stood at the opposite end of the corridor, two large manila envelopes in her hands.

Emmy strolled up to the cell. "Here." She pushed the manila envelopes through the bars. One was marked Frank Hardy, the other Joe Hardy.

"How'd you get our stuff?" Joe asked.

"I pulled in a lot of favors to get you two out of here," Emmy announced. She walked over to the steel door and pressed a button.

The cell lock clicked, and Frank pushed open the door. He and Joe headed for the steel door.

"Other way, guys," Emmy said, pointing behind them. "I don't think you want to run into Cronkite right now. He doesn't know you're getting out this early."

"Where's the tape?" Frank asked.

"It's on Cronkite's desk," Emmy explained. "I couldn't palm it with him sitting there."

"That tape is the only clue we have to Chet's location." Frank wadded his empty envelope and tossed it away.

"Sorry," Emmy said softly.

They followed Emmy through a series of hallways and then out a back door.

"Fresh air and sunshine." Joe breathed in deeply.

"You guys really need a bath," Emmy said, wrinkling up her nose.

"No time," Frank said as he adjusted his watch band. "We've got to get to Paradise Salvage."

"I know," Emmy said. "I heard Cronkite ranting and raving about your theory in the squad room. I tend to agree with him. The phone bills are not evidence that Chet is at Paradise Salvage. It does help my theory, however, that Smith was moving stolen parts through Max's place. Probably sending orders over that computer hotline."

"We've got to check out Paradise Salvage," Joe said.

"Yes," Emmy replied.

They walked on in silence for a few moments.

"Hey, where are we?" Joe suddenly asked.

Emmy had led the Hardys several blocks

from the police station to a large fenced-in parking lot. Dozens of cars, motorcycles, trucks, and other vehicles filled the area. A sign identified the place as the Southport P.D. Impound Complex.

"Your van won't be released for a couple more hours," Emmy said. "I thought perhaps you might need something from it."

"How are we going to raid Paradise Salvage without the van?" Joe asked, disappointment in his voice.

"We'll use my wheels," Emmy replied as she walked toward a small building. "I'll meet you two out front."

"Man, look at this damage," Joe groaned as they walked up to the van.

The van's armored siding had kept the shotgun blasts from piercing the van's shell but had left several sizable dents. Paint was blown away to reveal quarter-inch deep steel dimples.

While Joe inspected the damage, Frank grabbed a small tool box and another set of dark clothes. Then he and Joe walked to the front gate.

A low rumble caused Frank and Joe to turn. They were stunned by the sight of Emmy's car. A long, low, two-door, black-and-pink 1955 Buick pulled up beside the pair.

"Hop in," she yelled over the engine roar.

Frank recognized it as the restored Buick in

the photos. He opened the passenger door, pulled up the seat, and offered the backseat to Joe. Joe raised an eyebrow and reluctantly crawled in back.

Emmy peeled away from the curb.

"Does this dinosaur have a radio?" Joe asked.

"Sure," Emmy said, laughing. She flipped on the radio. A minute later, Buddy Holly belted out the driving rhythm of "Peggy Sue" through squeaky old speakers.

"Don't you have any newer tunes?" Joe asked over the speakers and the engine. "Say from this century."

"Sorry, Joe," Emmy replied. "This radio refuses to play anything other than fifties classics."

"Why are you doing all this for us?" Frank asked.

Emmy didn't answer for several moments. Then she said calmly, "I need your help. If we don't work together on this, you may never see your friend again, and I'll never bring my father's killer to justice."

The word *justice* hissed through Emmy's teeth like a snake ready to strike. She may have said justice, but the tone said *revenge*.

A chill raced down Frank's spine. Emmy was willing to sacrifice everything to find her father's killer—maybe even Chet.

"We should be at AutoHaus Emporium when the kidnapper calls at three," Frank suggested. He glanced at his watch. "It's one-thirty now. Meet us back at the motel room in an hour."

"Sounds good to me," Emmy replied.

Over an hour later, Emmy and the black-and-pink classic pulled up in front of the motel. Frank once again offered Joe the backseat.

"What took you so long?" Joe asked as Emmy peeled away from the motel.

"I stopped at the station and got a copy of the tape. Fortunately, Cronkite was out of the office." Emmy pulled out the tape and gave it to Frank.

"Thanks," Frank said.

Ten minutes later they strolled through the showroom of AutoHaus Emporium. They found Uncle Ed in his spacious office, his head in his hands. He jerked up as they entered the room, his eyes red and puffy, his face twisted in grief and worry.

"He just called," Uncle Ed gasped.

"Did you record it?" Joe asked.

"No. Somehow he found out about the answering machine. He threatened to kill Chet if I didn't shut off the tape."

Frank shot Emmy a knowing look. Cronkite had to be the mole in the police department.

"What did he say?" Frank asked.

"He wants the one hundred thousand dollars tonight—midnight—or he'll kill Chet." Uncle Ed sobbed. Then he rose and started out of the office. "I've got to get to the bank."

Joe grabbed the shaken man. "Did he say anything else? Where you could find Chet?"

Uncle Ed breathed deeply. "No. I just begged him not to hurt Chet. He only laughed and said his partner was meditating on it. *Please!* I've got to save Chet." Uncle Ed twisted away from Joe and stomped out of the office.

Frank jumped up and shouted, "That's it!"

Emmy and Joe were startled.

Frank dashed behind the desk and flipped on the power to Uncle Ed's stereo. Classical music erupted from the speakers.

"What are you doing?" Joe couldn't believe that Frank wanted to listen to music at a time like this.

"Something about that first phone call has been bugging me." He shoved the cassette into the tape player. "What did Uncle Ed just say? That the kidnapper's partner was meditating about killing Chet. Who do we know that meditates?"

"Max," Emmy replied quickly.

Frank punched the PLAY button and cranked up the volume. The speakers squealed.

"Frank!" Emmy yelled over the wail, her hands over her ears.

"Are you crazy?" Joe shouted.

The voices on the tape were a distorted jumble of booms and tweets. The hissing of static from the phone line sounded like rushing water. The pictures on the walls vibrated.

"Frank, *please!*" Emmy pleaded.

"Ssh!"

Frank turned down the bass to lower the voices and keep the speakers from humming. He adjusted the treble so the hissing and high tones weren't as distorted. He closed his eyes, his mind and ears tuned in on the sound that had bothered him for two days, the sound that hung in the background like a cloud in a fog.

The noise was faint, garbled, but distinctive—a steady, persistent humming and banging. A crushing sound.

"Hear it?" Frank asked.

"The crusher at Paradise Salvage!" Emmy yelled.

"Right!" Frank shut off the stereo.

An eerie silence filled the office.

"That meditating remark and the sound of the crusher are all the proof I need," Joe said, rubbing his ears.

"Cronkite will want to hear this," Emmy said, beaming at Frank. She reached for the phone.

Joe clamped his hand on the receiver. "You're not calling Cronkite."

Emmy's green eyes fired bullets at Joe. "Why not?"

"Someone's followed every move we make, even sent two killers after us. Until we know who, we keep our plans to ourselves."

"Cronkite is not a bad cop. There's a mole in the department, but it's not Cronkite. You have my word on it."

"Not good enough," Joe said.

"Cronkite was the only one who had enough faith in me to put me on this investigation."

"Perhaps he only did that to keep an eye on you," Joe said.

"Why would he need to do that?"

"In case you got close to finding your father's killer," Joe answered.

"Why should that bother Cronkite?"

"It wouldn't. Unless he was the one who killed your father."

Emmy's face became blank, her eyes round and confused. Joe could tell that the thought that Cronkite had killed her father had never crossed her mind. He felt a twinge of sympathy for her.

Emmy gazed at Frank.

"If he's a part of the chop shop gang, he would have had to get your father out of the way," Frank explained. "You said yourself they were friends. I never knew your father, but wouldn't he have reported a bad cop to the authorities?''

Emmy shuddered. "Okay. It's just us then. I'll be here tonight with Uncle Ed. You two find your friend at Paradise Salvage. I'll draw you a map." She turned and left the office.

"I didn't mean to shake her up that way," Joe said.

"She hasn't gotten over her father's death," Frank replied. "Would you?"

A sudden wave of awareness washed over Joe. Frank didn't have to explain any further. Joe knew that if he and Frank made one mistake during the raid on Paradise Salvage, Chet would end up dead.

Chapter
15

MIDNIGHT.

Frank and Joe crouched outside the tall chain-link fence on a back section of Paradise Salvage. The full moon showed through a chilling gray mist, causing an uneasy restlessness to surge through the Hardys.

Frank held two heavy-duty dog chains in his left hand and two pounds of hamburger in his right. Emmy had given them a detailed map of the junkyard.

The plan was simple. Either Max or Smith would have to stay at the salvage yard while the other met with Uncle Ed at AutoHaus Emporium. Emmy would be hidden and ambush the kidnapper who showed up for the money; Frank and Joe would surprise the other at Paradise Salvage and rescue Chet.

Frank's only real concern was the two mastiffs, Peace and Love. He hoped they would respond when he gave the Take-it-easy command. If that worked, the hamburger would be a friendly gesture while he and Joe chained the dogs to a stack of cars.

Frank pressed the light button on his watch and nodded to Joe.

Joe began snipping at the chain-link fence with a pair of bolt cutters.

No sooner had they crawled through the opening in the fence, than Peace and Love came rushing toward them, growling furiously.

"Take it easy!" Frank commanded.

The dogs halted and tilted their heads from side to side in confusion. Then they seemed to recognize Frank and wagged their tails and sat.

"Good dogs," Joe said. He took one chain from Frank.

Frank divided the hamburger and tossed it to the dogs. Peace and Love gulped down the meat.

"Good dog, Peace," Frank said. He clipped the chain to the dog's studded collar. Joe did the same to Love. They ran the chains through a smashed grill and around a bumper.

Frank pointed the way, and the Hardys jogged toward the shack. They approached the shack from the back side. It was a small one-room structure located in the middle of the salvage yard. Emmy had said that Max used the shack for extra storage and not much else. It was the most likely place for Chet to be held.

Surrounding the shack were dozens of large wrinkled metal cubes, the remains of cars compressed to two-foot squares by the crusher. In the moonlight, they looked like large square metal prunes.

The shack was dark, quiet. The Hardys moved slowly around to the front, their eyes and ears focused and tuned into the sights and sounds of the night.

Joe slowly rose and peered in through a window. He squinted. Several moments passed before he realized the window was painted black.

Frank put his hand on the doorknob and slowly turned. He cringed as the rusted latch creaked. He took a deep breath before opening the door. He hoped that the door's hinges were oiled.

He pushed the door in. He sighed as the hinges remained silent.

Frank and Joe crept inside and stood on either side of the door, away from the moonlit opening.

Joe pulled his penlight from his pocket and clicked it on.

They gasped.

The beam had fallen directly on Chet. He lay unconscious against the wall across the room.

His nose, cheeks, and lips were swollen and bruised.

Frank and Joe started heading for their friend when a sudden burst of light blinded them. Dark spots seemed to be floating in the air before them.

"Welcome to your nightmare," a cold voice said.

Frank recognized it as the voice from the tape. He rubbed his eyes and blinked. The room came into focus as his pupils adjusted to the light. He could once again make out the form of his unconscious friend.

On either side of Chet stood the two assassins from Skyway Parking Garage, Blackie and Red, in gray suits and sunglasses.

Blackie's .45 was aimed at Chet's head. Red's sawed-off semiautomatic shotgun covered the Hardys.

Both Frank and Joe noticed that Red's left pant leg had a small hole, a dark stain surrounding it.

Emmy stood next to Red, her arms crossed in front of her. "Don't move," she ordered.

Frank was too stunned, too angry to speak. *Betrayed!*

Despite the odds against them, Joe made a move toward Blackie. He wanted to distract the gunman, get him to turn his weapon away from Chet.

Red swung the shotgun on Joe. "Listen to the little lady," he growled in the same voice he used on the tape. He nodded at the floor.

Joe looked down. He and Frank were standing in a thin pool of water. Two bare copper wires ran from the water and were plugged into an electrical wall outlet. Blackie's free hand rested on the switch above the outlet.

"Over there with your friends," Red snarled. Using the barrel of the shortened shotgun, he shoved Emmy toward Frank and Joe.

Emmy slipped as she stepped into the water. She broke her fall by putting her crossed hands on Frank's chest. Frank noticed that her hands were tied.

"Quite the gentleman, huh, Frank Hardy?" Red sneered. "I knew who you were when that chick cop brought you in here." Red's gloating smile spread the width of his face.

He pulled the red wig from his head, his long gray hair falling to his shoulders. He tossed it to the floor, followed by the sunglasses. Max Elburk's smile was venomous.

"You three were becoming real pains in the neck for my partner and me," Blackie said. He pulled off his black wig and sunglasses.

"Butch!" Joe cried out.

Frank questioned Emmy with his eyes.

"Butch was waiting for me when I arrived at AutoHaus," Emmy said.

"Cronkite in on this?" Frank asked.

"Cronkite?" Max laughed. "That loud-mouth yahoo wouldn't know how to be dishonest."

"You're not getting away with this," Joe warned.

"Yeah. You expecting the marines to come and rescue you or something?" Max sneered. "I know you three are alone in this."

"How?" Emmy asked.

"You cops don't pay your dispatchers enough," Max explained, grinning.

"The mole is a dispatcher?" Frank asked, staring hard at Emmy.

"I left word with the dispatcher to contact Cronkite, in case something happened," Emmy explained.

"Exactly," Max drawled. "You should have sold Butch the garage when you had the chance, Emmy," Max said. "You would have at least gotten some money out of it. Now it looks as though we'll pick up Royce's Garage at a bargain price."

"How's that?" Emmy asked, hate in her eyes.

"At the estate sale, after your sudden but tragic accident—just like your father's."

"Only the killer would know how my father died."

"Yeah. That's right," Max said, cackling.

137

"You're *dead!*" Emmy screamed.

She jumped at Max so quickly that Frank didn't have time to grab her and Max didn't have time to move. Emmy slammed into Max, knocking him against the wall. The shotgun fell to the floor.

Frank and Joe made a move for the shotgun.

"Don't move!" Smith shouted, his hand on the switch.

Emmy hit Max in the stomach with her tied fists, and he doubled over. She raised her hands above her head and was ready to strike down on Max's neck when the sudden roar of a gun being discharged into the roof filled the shack.

Smith then brought his .45 down and leveled it at Chet's head, cocking back the hammer. Smoke still streamed from the barrel.

"Back off or Morton's dead," Smith threatened through clenched teeth.

Emmy stared at Smith, then looked down at Max.

"Emmy," Frank said sternly.

Emmy turned toward Frank, her green eyes flashing. Her face twisted with rage and pain.

Frank was prepared to attack Emmy if she didn't back away from Max. He wasn't going to let her put his friend's life in jeopardy.

"You wouldn't be able to live with Chet's death," Frank said.

Emmy lowered her arms, walked over to Frank, and then stood beside him. Frank could tell she was fighting back tears.

Max picked up the shotgun and stood up. "Seems Emmy's the only brave one among you," he sneered, holding his stomach.

"Let's toast them now," Butch said with a grin.

"What about Chet?" Joe asked.

Max looked down at the unconscious Chet. "He doesn't know who we are or where he's been since Sunday. He's only seen us in these disguises. He's our insurance that good old Uncle Ed doesn't call the cops until we feel it's safe," Max replied. "You three, however, know who we are."

"I still say we get rid of Fat Boy now," Butch growled. He kicked Chet's feet. Chet groaned.

"Try that with me, jerk," Joe threatened.

Max laughed. Then to Butch he said, "That's why you're not the brains. We need Fat Boy, even if he is uncooperative. Now, let's party, partner."

"Show time!" Butch shouted.

He brought his hand down in one grand swooping gesture toward the lethal switch.

Chapter

16

CHET MORTON suddenly came to life. He lashed out with a vicious kick that connected with Butch's kneecap.

Butch howled in pain as he toppled backward, his hand missing the switch and flipping off the overhead light switch instead, plunging the room into darkness.

Frank, Joe, and Emmy separated as the shotgun erupted, followed quickly by the .45. The room was lit by the red-yellow muzzle flash of both weapons.

Frank scrambled to the opposite side of the room. His plan was to make his way around the edge of the wall and come up on the side of Max.

A sudden wooden crash caused him to freeze. Moonlight streamed in as the rear door burst open. Butch darted through the door, followed by a limping Max.

"I'll get the light!" Frank shouted.

"Wait!" Joe warned. He clicked on his pen-light. "You might hit the wrong switch." He aimed his light at the two wall switches. "The one on the right."

"Thanks, Joe." Frank hit the switch and the room was once again washed in the yellowish glow of the low-watt bulb.

Joe knelt next to a groggy Chet. "Welcome back from the dead," he said with a smile.

"Yeah. Thanks," Chet grunted.

Using his pocketknife, Joe cut the cords around Chet's wrists and ankles while Frank loosened the rope holding Emmy's hands.

"How do you feel, buddy?" Frank asked.

Chet stood with Joe's help, his rubbery legs wobbling beneath him. He had to lean on Joe to keep from falling. "I've been tied up like that since Sunday night. They knocked me out again just before they left to meet Uncle Ed, but that gun blast woke me up. I pretended to be passed out. I knew you two would need my help."

"Thanks. I thought we were fried," Frank said, indicating the water and wire.

"Butch and Max are getting away," Joe said, ignoring Frank's comment. He scanned the stacks of flattened cars from the open back door.

"Well, they're not escaping," Emmy announced. "The only gate is the one next to the house and parts barn. They took off in the wrong direction. They're going to have to circle around to escape. You can cut them off before they reach it. I'll call Cronkite for backup."

"Like the man said," Frank began as he dashed to the front door, "it's show time."

The Hardys dashed out into the night. The full moon provided enough light to allow them to see clearly up and down the rows of stacked flattened cars. The stacks provided dark shadowy hiding places for the Hardys—and for Max and Butch.

"They're going to have to circle around to the north side," Frank said, visualizing the map in his mind. "Max's leg wound ought to slow them down."

They stopped and pressed themselves against a stack of cars. Frank poked his head around the corner and then back into the shadows. Nothing, he shook his head at Joe. They crouched and sprinted across the open lane.

"Let's put the odds a little more in our favor," Joe said, looking up.

"What's your plan?"

"Climb up on the next row, ambush them as they walk by."

Frank liked Joe's idea. The last thing they needed to do was meet the two men in the open. They sprinted to the next row of stacked cars and climbed up the fifteen-foot-high stack, avoiding loose chrome, side mirrors, and other car parts that might creak and give away their position.

Once on top, they lay down and leaned over the edge just enough to see down the lane. It was empty.

Frank couldn't have been wrong. This was the only way they could get to the gate. Perhaps they had doubled back, headed for the shack—for Emmy and Chet!

Joe nudged Frank and pointed. Frank strained to see in the direction his brother was pointing. A dark outline limped slowly in the shadows of the stack across from them, a shotgun held waist level. Max.

Where was Butch?

Frank moved forward slightly and leaned over the edge. Butch was directly below him, the .45 held straight in front of him, its hammer locked back.

Frank scooted back from the edge. He nudged Joe, pointed down, then held up one finger.

Joe nodded that he understood.

Frank leaned forward. A rusted chunk of metal gave way and creaked.

A thunderous roar fragmented the silence. Shotgun pellets spattered the edge of the stack in front of Frank and Joe.

The Hardys rolled away from the edge and then dropped to the opposite side of the stacked flattened cars.

"The other side!" they heard Max yell.

A second later Butch appeared at the head of the lane, his .45 spitting fire and lead.

Frank and Joe ducked and sprinted toward the back of the salvage yard, .45 slugs whistling past them. They came to a break in the row, Frank diving to the left, Joe to the right.

"You're dead, Hardys! *Dead!*" Butch screamed.

"Butch?" Max yelled.

"Yeah, over here," Butch answered. "They're cornered like trapped rats."

Butch was right. Frank and Joe were safe, but only until Max and Butch could walk to the break in the row.

"Come out, come out wherever you are," Max said, cackling.

They *were* trapped. They could climb over the stacks, but Max and Butch would still be on the loose, hunting them down between the rows of dead cars.

144

"Hey, Hardys!" Max shouted. "Need any spare parts?"

Joe seized a hubcap lying next to his foot. He held it up for Frank to see and made a throwing motion.

Frank nodded that he understood. He held up three fingers. Joe gave him the okay sign.

Joe stepped away from the stack and held the hubcap like a Frisbee.

Frank raised his fist, counted three with his fingers, and jumped into the lane.

"Hey, creeps!" he shouted.

Max and Butch swung their weapons at Frank and fired.

Frank dove back behind the stack, bullets and pellets tearing away at the metal edge.

Joe jumped out. His arm uncoiled like a tightly compressed spring and the hubcap slashed through the air in a straight line for Butch. The chrome disk caught Butch in the forehead with a metallic *thwack*. Butch reeled as though he had been shot and slammed into the stack of cars. He bounced off and collapsed on the ground.

Joe leapt back into the niche as Max pumped the shotgun and fired off several rounds.

Then all was silent.

Frank and Joe looked at each other. Moments passed and still no sound.

Frank took a chance and leaned out, quickly

ducking back. Except for Butch's motionless body, the lane was empty. He signaled to Joe and they crept out slowly, keeping their eyes at the end of the row, in case Max was hiding.

They made their way to Butch. Frank kicked the .45 away, knelt down, and lifted the chopper's wrist.

"Still breathing," Frank announced as he dropped the arm. He pointed to Butch's bleeding forehead. "But he'll have a headache when he wakes up."

Joe picked up the .45 and pressed the clip release. The clip fell into his hand and he looked inside it.

"Empty," he said, tossing the gun and the clip to the side.

Frank patted Butch's pockets. "No ammo here. Any ideas?" Frank asked.

Joe knelt down and pinched a spot of dark soil. He rubbed his fingers and the dirt became a sticky paste. "Blood," he announced. "All this running around must have reopened the wound Emmy gave him."

Frank and Joe followed the speckled trail of blood. They were surprised that Max hadn't gone toward the gate but headed farther back into the twisted maze of stacked, flattened cars.

The trail led to the rear of the salvage yard.

The drops became smaller and soon disappeared altogether.

Frank and Joe moved slowly, every nerve in their bodies on edge, every muscle tense.

They neared the back section where they had cut through the fence. Something clanked behind them and they spun around, expecting to see Max.

"Oldest trick in the book and you two dead dudes fall for it," Max sneered.

They whirled around. It was obvious that Max had thrown something to distract them. Now he stood in front of them, the shotgun at his waist, pointing at Frank and Joe.

Peace and Love obediently sat on either side of Max, their chains on the ground. Max made a twisting motion with his hand toward Frank and Joe.

Peace and Love stood, black lips pulled back over yellow razor-sharp teeth.

Max gave a second silent signal—a clinched fist—and the dogs crept forward, heads lowered, fur on end, evil growls rising from deep within their throats.

The Hardys remained still.

"Hey!" Frank shouted. Then more calmly, "Take it easy."

The two dogs straightened up, wagged their tails, then bounced toward the Hardys as though they were all long-lost friends.

"Good boy," Joe said as he patted Love on the head.

"It's over, Max," Frank said.

"No!" Max raised the shotgun and pulled the twin triggers of both barrels.

Frank and Joe didn't have time to dive out of the way.

The hammers hit the striking plate with a weak click. The shotgun was empty.

Max threw the shotgun at the Hardys, but the gun fell short. He limped to the fence and tried to squeeze through the opening. His jacket and pants caught on the jagged edges of the cut chain link, nearly impaling him.

"Going somewhere?" Chet asked. Aided by Emmy, he hobbled toward Frank and Joe. "Thanks, Emmy. I can handle it from here."

Chet straightened up to his full height and walked toward Max. With both hands he pulled the cowering man back through the fence, ripping Max's gray suit. Max squirmed, but Chet's viselike clamp prevented him from escaping.

"No one calls *me* Fat Boy and gets away with it," Chet snarled.

With the speed, accuracy, and power of a professional boxer, Chet planted his square, broad fist on Max's chin.

Max groaned, stumbled against the fence, and slid to the ground.

Chapter
17

"WHAT'S TAKING HER SO LONG?" Joe asked. He peered out the window and glanced up and down the street.

"Staring out the window won't get Emmy here any quicker," Frank said as he returned from the kitchen with a tray of lemonade and placed it on the table. He sat on the couch next to Callie and began pouring a glass for Chet, who sat on the loveseat across from them.

Joe turned away from the window and threw himself into an overstuffed chair.

"I don't know why you talked me into letting Emmy patch up the van. We could have gotten one of the repair shops in Bayport to fix it."

"Emmy's price was right," Frank said. He handed the glass of lemonade to Chet. "Free."

"If it was your computer, you wouldn't let

anybody less than an expert look at it," Joe said.

"From what I've heard," Callie began, "this Emerson Sauter is an expert." Callie took a glass of lemonade from Frank. "Isn't she, Frank?"

Frank ignored Callie's remark and turned to Chet. "When Emmy called to say she was returning the van today, she said that Butch had pleaded guilty to car theft and operating a chop shop, and he's turning state's evidence against Max. He doesn't want to be tried for the two murders that Max committed—Snake and Royce Sauter. That plus your testimony will put both of them away for a long time."

"Life plus eternity would be too short," Chet replied.

"The next time my parents go on a cruise, I'm staying home where I can be part of the action," Callie said over the top of her glass.

"And keep an eye on Frank," Joe added, grinning.

Frank frowned at Joe.

"Did they recover the computer?" Chet asked.

"Yes," Frank replied. "Smith had it in the trunk of the old woman's sports car. They plugged it in and were able to print out all of Smith and Elburk's transactions. According to

Emmy, over sixty stolen car cases have been linked to them.''

"Didn't you say Emerson was young and single?" Callie asked.

Frank sighed. He didn't know what Joe and Chet had told Callie about Emmy, but he knew that they had exaggerated. He was about to explain this to Callie when a horn suddenly blared out front.

"The van!" Joe shouted. He jumped from his chair and bolted out the front door.

He came to a sudden, stunned stop.

The van looked showroom new. The black paint was deeper, richer, and so highly polished that it was like a black mirror, reflecting everything around it with crystal clarity.

"Not bad, huh?" Emmy hopped from the van.

Joe could only gawk. He walked slowly around the van, running his hands over the areas where the shotgun pellets had left dents and scars. The sides were glass smooth, and Joe couldn't tell where Emmy had used body putty.

"Hi, Frank," Emmy said as Frank, Callie, and Chet walked up to the van. "You're looking better, Chet."

"Thanks," Chet said.

"Emmy, this is Callie Shaw," Frank said nervously.

"Hi," Callie said. Frank could tell Callie was trying to make up her mind about Emmy.

"Hi," Emmy said. "Frank's told me about you."

"I'll bet he did," Callie said a little coolly.

"You're pretty lucky to have such a loyal boyfriend," Emmy said. "I asked him out, but he turned me down. Can you believe it?"

"Well, I, uh, guess so," Callie replied, confused. She turned to Frank.

Frank felt his face blush and suppressed a smile. Instead, he shrugged at Callie.

"So? Are you satisfied?" Emmy asked as Joe rejoined the group.

"Satisfied? This is fantastic," Joe replied.

"Thanks," Emmy said.

"We're going out for pizza," Callie said. "Would you like to join us?"

"Sure," Emmy replied.

"We're taking the van," Joe announced firmly. He handed Emmy the keys to the old Buick she had lent them. "For two weeks when I've driven that tank around, all my friends have called it the Pink Bayport Dinosaur." He hopped into the van's driver's seat and turned on the ignition. "Now I'm going to cruise to some modern tunes."

He flipped on the radio and cranked up the volume.

"Warden threw a party in the county jail!"

Elvis Presley yelled through the speakers as the beginning strains of "Jailhouse Rock" shook the air.

"*Yeow!*" Joe yelled. He jumped from the front seat and stared in confusion at his beloved van. "It's haunted!"

Frank, Callie, Chet, and Emmy burst out laughing.

Frank laughed even harder as Emmy leaned closer to him and whispered, "I wonder how long it'll be before he figures out that I've left my Presley tape in the cassette player?"

Frank and Joe's next case:

When an ultrasecret project takes Fenton Hardy to Massachusetts, the Hardy boys come home one afternoon to find that kidnappers have taken their mother. The kidnappers demand to talk to Frank and Joe's father within twenty-four hours—or the boys may never talk to their mother again.

The key to the case is at Prometheus Computing, where Fenton is in charge of security. The company's latest product is a highly advanced computer chip sure to shape the future of artificial intelligence. But to protect the chip and their family, the Hardys will have to rely on their natural intelligence and courage . . . in *Danger Zone*, Case #37 in The Hardy Boys Casefiles℠.